HALLELUJAH

by Liz Shine

Published in the United States by Red Dress Press.
http://reddresspress.net
http://lizshine.com

ISBN 978-0-9974670-1-7

Cover design by Emelita Trier, based on a photograph by Bobbi Rock-Petrocci

First printing August 2016

For my parents, Michael and Ann.

Acknowledgments

There are so many people to acknowledge for their support and encouragement during the many drafts and phases of making this book. I thank teachers and mentors: Lynne Lerych, David Huddle, and Jim Heynen, most prominently. I thank writer friends who read my work and advised me along the way: Chris D, Manek, Laura, Natalie, and Kristina. Love and gratitude to my husband, Chris, who edited, edited again, then edited some more. Holly, whose feedback and insight as an early reader exceeded my expectations so much that I may never be satisfied with early reader feedback again. Carrie, who read multiple drafts, provided excellent feedback, and is one of my most trustworthy cheerleaders. Everyone who ever asked me how the book was coming along after hearing the passage I read as part of my creative thesis when I graduated from the Rainier Writers Workshop, especially the few who said, "I still think about that character." There were times when I had to dig deep into my bag of faith to carry on. I sometimes found a comment like that there, and it served to push me forward. Thanks to all my family and friends who encourage me to keep writing, and especially my little sister who not only served as a reader early on, but who also designed a beautiful cover for Eve's story.

"We are our own dragons as well as our own heroes, and we have to rescue ourselves from ourselves."

Tom Robbins, *Still Life With Woodpecker*

ONE.

A person can drown in water, their own phlegm, or any substance other than air that fills up the lungs. We say we are drowning when we are not, because anything that stops the breath from moving freely *is* a kind of drowning. *Oh, my god! I'm drowning,* we think and say. We can drown in sorrow. We can drown in fear. Drown flailing in our own raucous desire.

Drowning fascinates me not only because I actually drowned twice, but also because of its connection to breath, the most important function of self we never think about. There are many ways to drown, many ways to swim, all of them connected to breath and practice.

I remember the first time I drowned in sketch, some details filled in over the years by imagination and others' stories.

Felt like four hours in a crowded station wagon: Mom, the

neighbor kids and their mom, my brother Noah and me. A hot day for Hoquiam, one of those days that remind you this earth can melt you down for any reason at all, or none. As the thermometer crept past one hundred, we fled to the Wynoochee River with our inner tubes and swimsuits and bags of food for barbecue.

The boys stretched their legs out in the backseat, trading coveted baseball cards. The girls sat piled in back, including Kate, who mostly ignored everyone, save a half smile of acceptance when Amy or I said or did something too funny to resist. Looking back, it seems we placed so much worth in Kate's half smiles, offered reluctantly, near-shielded by the novel she held in both hands.

And I think I know why.

Kate held mystery and promise for Amy and me, foreshadowed changes that would happen someday, maybe soon, when me might write love letters and begin to say things like *I'm going to be a lawyer*, the way Kate did as if fact was fact. At the time, my interest in Kate felt only like fascination (or even admiration) that had nothing to do with me. She had storm-blue eyes and dark brown hair that hung past her waist in waves. She had new curves and a fiery, determined pout, a lack of interest in the antics of little girls. We could not help studying Kate back then. And now, trying to tell the story of my own becoming, she emerges and belongs. How does one become the woman one is bound to be?

Through so many influences and increments.

Amy and I ran through every song we could remember the words
to and told every joke we knew between us and asked the boys stupid
questions like did they have girlfriends to which they said *No, ewwww*. We
asked Kate what she was reading, to which she replied matter-of-factly, *a
story about a girl who leaves home to avenge the death of her father.*

After a pause, I (or maybe Amy) asked, "Do you like it?"

"I love it!" She told us how she had read everything else the
author wrote. Seven or so books she counted on her fingers as she
named them. She loved them the way I loved *Charlotte Sometimes* and *Tales
of A Fourth Grade Nothing*, so I told her so, and she gave me that look
older kids give you when they have grown tired of you and you have said
something childish.

Mom turned up the car radio, and pretty soon the girls in the
back and the moms up front were singing "Young Hearts, Run Free,"
the way we did to songs we all knew the words to. Mom tapped her knee
with the palm of her hand and nodded her head, all of us shooting each
other knowing glances on our favorite lines. Even Kate joined in, though
at first she said she could not sing.

Noah made gagging gestures and Ben hit his hand on his chest
in that way boys did when they thought something was girly or just plain

stupid.

"It's so hot!" Noah said, plopping back in his seat.

Mom could not say, as she usually did, to roll down a window. All rolled down already, the wing windows popped open too, had no cooling effect. Noah hung his head out the window, an attempt to get free of the song and to cool off.

"It's like we're stuck in a giant dryer," Ben said, rolling from side to side in his seat, his face mock-anguished.

"We're almost there," Mom said, but no one believed her because that is what she always said. Almost there could mean anything. Almost there could be around the corner or all the way to Mexico, for all we knew. Almost there, almost done, almost heaven. Mom filled her glass half full and therefore could not be trusted with the truth.

"You'll be swimming in no time," she added, twisting in her seat to offer a perk-up-or-shut-up smile.

We wore our swimsuits under our clothes. Back in the driveway, before we left, Kate's mom nearly made her change.

"Where did you get that bikini?"

"Dad bought it for me last weekend."

Kate's dad had moved in with another woman over a year ago.

"Go put a one-piece on or at least a T-shirt over, not that half shirt you're wearing."

Kate shot her Mom a disdainful look that made us all turn away.

"Mom, it's hot! Why do I need more clothes? Besides, this is comfortable."

Kate's mom glanced side to side for help, apparently found none. *Fine, just get in the car.*

Kate bounded back to the car. Mom called Noah and Ben from where they faced off with stick swords they had picked off the lawn. She steered me by the shoulder to the car.

"Let's go," Kate's mom said, buckling her seat belt, donning her shades. I saw her glance at Kate stretched out in the back, triumphant. Was it fear on her face? Anger? Jealousy? I could not be sure, but I saw the piercing look and how Kate ignored it.

"We're here!" Noah yelled as Mom pulled onto a gravel road marked by a brown and yellow state park sign. The car rocked over the gravel.

"Looks like a lot of people had the same idea we did," Kate said, crinkling her nose.

Mom groaned, presumably at the fact that she had to park along the entry to the parking area—off the side of the road. As the car came to a stop, we poised for our escape. We bolted out doors and climbed over seats, but did not get very far. The Moms called us back for a lecture on how they were not going to carry everything for everyone and what did we think they looked like anyway? We mumbled our apologies and each of us grabbed something to carry.

We found a picnic spot close to the water, which made Mom happy and us too because we could throw our stuff down and scamper to the water in no time.

The sun beat down and the rocks were hot to walk over. Kate took an inner tube way out in the river. Her long pale body draped over the tube, her arms and legs splashing, her face skyward. Noah and Ben waded out, Noah carrying Ben's football and bragging about how he could throw a tight spiral. Amy and I took our buckets to collect rocks and those tiny, dark fish that swim in the mud.

Last time we went to the river it was just Noah and me, so he did not mind hanging back at the edge of the water teaching me how to skip rocks. Amy kept taking the rocks I found to make pieces of her mud castle and trying to make rules about what to do with the water we filled our buckets with, which annoyed me. I decided to skip rocks instead and relished the idea of throwing a nice flat rock before Amy could claim it.

I watched the boys out in the water, envious.

"Noah, Look!" I called, wanting to show him tricks I learned on my own.

No answer.

"Noah, look!" I tried again, choosing a real flat one.

No answer.

I walked up to see what the Moms were doing. They were leaned in, talking, the smell of cooking meat telling me they had settled us in for the day. Bags unpacked, cooler full, they prepared food for when we emerged from the water at our various times, hungry from play.

"Uh-Oh," Mom said as I approached. "What's eatin' you?"

"I'm bored," I said, plopping down on the bench, arms folded over my chest, heels banging against the cooler full of Shasta.

"Only boring people get bored," she said.

"I'm not boring!" I hated when she said that. I scrunched up my face, kicked the cooler hard with one heel, then the other.

"Are you hungry?" She stood, turning the dogs on the barbecue.

I nodded yes. Mom lightly tugged one pigtail and I smiled, but then went back to brooding. I took a hot dog with only ketchup and headed back to the river, eyes tracking the boys way out in the water.

"Noah, look!" I skipped the flattest rock I could find with my one free hand.

No answer.

I waded closer and tried again.

Still closer, hot dog held high.

From a reservoir in the Olympics, the Wynoochee flows to the Chehalis. Rivers move the water to the sea, where the water evaporates into rain, falls back into the cycle again. We drew pictures of this cycle for science class once. Our teacher tacked them on the wall, each one a little different, each one the same, titled *The Water Cycle*. My cow looked like a dog. My raincloud frowned. I mottled my sun with flecks of orange, red, and yellow.

The moment the river swept me under I saw the fireball sun, the evergreen sentinels surrounding us, the rare blue sky.

I have heard drowning is supposed to hurt, but I do not remember feeling pain. I remember significant silence and spinning, spinning, spinning, the water turning cold, colder as I sunk. I remember flashes of white light, dark hair fanning out—white legs—as Kate swooped in to save me.

Delivered back to shore, I coughed water out my mouth and nose.

"Are you okay?" All the color gone from Mom's face, she held my shoulders tight.

Was I dead?

"She's awake and breathing." Panic in Mom's voice.

Mom held me on her lap the rest of the afternoon telling me stories about her childhood like the time she punched a boy for saying there was no Santa Claus and how she loved to spend entire afternoons sitting on the branch of a maple tree in her front yard.

She sang *You Are My Sunshine*, her mouth curving into a smile and her eyes yessing me on You. I drank three lemon-lime sodas and ate all the chips I wanted. She braided my hair and let me try on her mirrored sunglasses.

The second time I nearly drowned, I was eleven and still had not learned to swim. I had come to the river that day with Mindy's parents. I did not know then I was in the twilight of that friendship. As friends do, I felt certain Mindy and I would always be sitting on picnic blankets by rivers, drinking sugary beverages together, eating hot dogs, whispering our secrets in trade. *You tell me one, I'll tell you.* Mindy had to repeat kindergarten, plus she was a fall baby, so in just a few months she would turn thirteen. She was preparing for that day. She reclined, propped on her elbows, her new breasts accented. She wore a white neon paint-splashed bikini with little bows on each hip. She crossed one leg over the other, settled onto her elbows, her sunglasses shielding the fact that she observed every movement of a group of boys looking for a lost frisbee in the woods near the shore.

When their frisbee landed on our blanket, she snatched it up and waited.

"Sorry about that." The tallest, tannest boy approached.

"It's cool." She still held the frisbee, turn-tossing it in her hand.

"Can we have it back?"

"If you tell me your name," she said.

He laughed. "Kevin, and that's Jake and Joe."

Mindy handed over the frisbee. "I'm Mindy, and this is Eve."

I flushed. The sun seemed hotter, brighter. I squinted my eyes to look up at him, managed a cracked hello.

Mindy gave no warning before she dove into the water. She walked up to the edge of the river, took two quick steps, aimed her arms out, palms together and dove her body to where it was deep enough to swim.

I stayed for a while watching as she swam out to the huddle of kids on the woods side of the river, away from the parent side, the shore. Mindy knew I could not swim, but maybe she forgot. I had not told her parents.

I waded out, the chill river water bathing my feet. I waded closer, drawn to their chatter, the laughter that reached to the tops of the trees, the splashing of legs and arms, the occasional self-baptism as one of them held their nose and dove under, then up again, shaking the water off.

They call it a drop off.

One step your feet are on the ground and then—no ground.

Kevin saw my flailing arms, heard my cries, and saved me. He pulled me onto his inner tube and swam me to shore. *Oh, my god, you nearly drowned. I think I might have saved you. I didn't mean to, I just did.*

Just a guess, but that is how I heard what he did not say.

I have returned in my memory to those near-drownings again and again, only vaguely aware of their most important aspect. I have written that it was the brush with death itself, that particular loss of innocence. I have written that it was Kate, so self-assured, and how she left a memory trace I could build on if I wanted to. Was it Noah and the distance

between us? Was it the heat of the day? Was it the look of fear on Mom's

face when I came to? Was it Kevin and his saving me?

My near drownings do not compare to the ones that came after,

the ones that were not about staying afloat in water but were a kind of

drowning nonetheless, were also about movement and breath in spite

of the brain and fear. What I want to show you is how I learned to save

myself, how it had everything to do with movement.

TWO.

For a day or two after my first brush with death, Mom regarded me as she did eggs in her shopping cart, with just a little more care and attention. With more generosity, too: sweets before bed, lights-out negotiable. But before long and without ceremony, our lives settled into what they had been before, the ripple of my near-drowning smoothed by habit and necessity.

Mom studied from breakfast to story time, pensive. She worried that on top of her nursing courses she needed to get a job. She fretted about finding babysitters and making payments. She missed Dad, who had left for reasons she did not talk about at the time. She would stretch the long cord of the telephone across the room and close her bedroom door. Until there was no telephone, and we started spending Sundays at the Coin-Op Laundromat because a frowning man in overalls came to take our dryer away.

Frank ran the laundromat. His wife, Grace, filled dry-cleaning orders in the back. He always had a joke like *What do you call two monkeys in a Corvette?* or *Knock, Knock* and Grace, smiling, shook her head in gentle reproof. He made change for the gumball machine, the soap dispenser, the washers and dryers, and attended to complaints about lost quarters.

Noah raced his toy cars across the tiles or played pinball. I watched people come and go, read Boxcar Children mysteries, and helped Mom keep track of loads of laundry and fold clothes into perfect piles. I figured life could go on that way forever, too young to understand the thread we clung to, to understand the need for the plan Mom was hatching to save us.

The morning of my eighth birthday, evidence from the previous night's rain storm lay strewn across the yard: branches from our hemlock tree, an empty milk carton and frozen dinner package from the neighbor's garbage can. A gray day, still drizzling, the kind you get used to when you live somewhere where two-thirds of all your days happen under gray-cloudy skies.

I did not make much of Mom's tearful goodbye that morning when she dropped Noah and me off at Granny and Grampa's house for a family party she either was not invited to or did not want to attend. She often cried. I assumed she would pick us up some hours later, when I would have an armful of presents, and be stuffed with German chocolate cake (my favorite and promised to me by Granny).

Afterward, years later, I would peruse the memory for the cues I missed. The way you poke a bruise you know still hurts just to remind yourself *how* it hurts.

The week before there had been a note taped to the door when we got home. The note had knocked Mom's manic mood off-kilter, broke open the floodgates of her sorrow. She would get that way sometimes, teary. She would pull me closer and closer to her body, pressing me to her, touching my hair, wiping my face with her saliva-doused thumb. She would say *I should just kill myself* as if she could take it back later, but she could not ever entirely take it back. That sentence uttered by a mother is indelible.

In response to the note she made a secret plan, the only plan she could make. She did not tell us, she would say later, because she could not bear to. This was a ripping off the bandage situation. She felt she could lessen the hurt by containing it inside her.

She was wrong.

The day she left us, she did not even call until two days later.

Crying, she asked, "How are you?" Her refrain *You know I love you, honey* over and over again followed with each question I asked.

"Why?"

"It's only for a while."

"How long?"

"I don't know. Not long."

"How long is not long?"

Nothing allowed me to fill in the gaps of missing information that might help me understand why Mom dropped us off, planning to not pick us up, why she had concealed her plan.

She did not have a choice, she said. The eviction notice forced her hand. It was only for a while. These are things she told me, but I could not understand. I would live with Dad and Noah would live with Granny and Grampa, *only for a little while*, she promised again and again.

She came by later the day of the phone call to drop off our things. Her friend waited in the car, engine running. I sat on the wood-planked porch steps to wave goodbye and she kept leaving and coming back for one more hug.

Who was this Dad? Mom cried and cried for his leaving. She never said a mean word about him. Memories from that time are puzzle pieces I would spend years trying to make fit. Images from memory emerge and somehow make my portrait of father, incomplete as it is: looking out our window watching Noah and the neighbor kids play in what seemed to me like heaps of snow, me pouting from the warmth of my living room because Mom and Dad said I was too little to join the others., watching through the glass: only snow, covering everything, mid-day darkness, thick indoor air; Dad sitting in the chair, reading, his feet propped on a glass-top coffee table, his wire-framed glasses falling down on his nose; Dad getting into a car and driving away; Dad making Tang with four ice cubes each for me and Noah.

I cannot even be sure these memories are real. According to some, I was too young to have memories. Had I constructed them from their stories or are they real snapshots, moments preserved between stretches of forgetting?

Dad left in summer. Mom described the getaway car with ire, a brown pinto. Dad liked men, had always liked men, Mom explained and tried to hide the disgust in her voice, cover it up with more stories about how he was so kind, her friend.

They were best friends. Though Mom has fluctuated on whether and where she attended church, she has always looked skyward for salvation. Dad had a vision or something that made him suddenly believe (though he had never set foot in a church before). At one point in her recollection of this story, Mom let it slip that hallucinogens played a part. Mom believed with such zeal. Dad felt sure she could help him keep his faith, that marriage could save him. They had wed in an acid-encouraged God-promise to save each other from sinning. Mom wanted Dad. Dad wanted to be straight for salvation's sake.

Six when Dad left, I had almost no memories of my own, a few borrowed memories and a lot of confusion about who he was and why he left. And yet, here I was, going to live with him. *For a while.*

With just the two of us living together, he opened himself to me in a way he never would again. We lived in this two-story overlooking downtown Olympia and Budd Bay. When I think of that home, I smell marijuana, low tide, and Dad's specialty grilled cheese sandwiches. Feed yourself, he seemed to say. Follow your heart. I see Dad sitting in his sunroom cross-legged, meditating, which seemed a lot like Mom when she prayed, only quieter.

Even the strange did not seem so strange. A July afternoon spent swimming with a dozen or so grown men, for instance. All of them naked, their cocks hanging out like jewelry. Dad among them. The smell of grass. Birds twittering and moving in tight cliques. Blue sky with dollops of fat, white clouds. Naked—old, fat, thin, young. What did all these men have in common that they would come here together, shed their clothes, loll in the sun, splash in the swimming hole, stand-kissing behind the transparent veil of the water falls?

I knew Dad was gay, but seeing it did not mesh with what I thought that meant. Coming from Mom's mouth, gay sounded like other words I knew: whore, lazy, bad influence. Now, gay sounded like the sun glimmering on the surface of a pond, like men, naked, laughing together. My tall, smiling-eyed, dark-haired Dad? His laugh, quick and full of knowing. There did not seem to be anything bad about him.

I cannot say what possessed him to bring me, an eight-year-old girl, swimming that day, but it was not perversion. It seems still the best effort he has ever made to explain himself to me. Dad came out before coming out was cool. To be outside of the norm will always carry a burden, but in my lifetime I have seen that burden lessen for young men and women who love within their gender. It must be both exhilarating and maddening to look at the world and wonder what if you had just been born too early? So much suffering has to do with circumstances of birth. It would have been difficult to be gay and be Dad. Taking me swimming that day felt like an act of courage, a willingness to be himself around me.

I wanted pierced ears, but was afraid. He said *look, I have my ears pierced and my nipples, too. It's not so bad.* Then, he took me to his friend Patty, who pierced ears and other parts for a living.

"Hop up," she said, patting the stool I would sit on. It was one of those stools with a lever that moves the cushy vinyl seat up or down.

Patty had long orange-red hair, teased and sprayed, and she wore a camisole, straps falling off her shoulders.

"Who's that?" I asked, pointing to a picture of a little girl in pigtails.

"That's my baby."

The girl had Patty-red hair and several missing teeth in her not-camera-shy grin. Behind me, inspecting my ears in the mirror, Patty pulled on one earlobe, then the other, then both.

"What's her name?" I asked.

"Veronica." Pause. "I think she'd like you." She pierced both ears while she spoke, finished after "you".

"Maybe we could play some time," I said, wincing at the sting, noticing the tattoo on Patty's arm that said *Remember* in fancy lettering across a true red heart.

"What a brave girl you are," Patty said, the palm of her hand smoothed the middle of my back.

Yes, brave, I thought, and felt taller. Dad took me out to ice cream and I ordered black licorice on a sugar cone. It tasted like sweet tears.

Every day in Olympia felt new. We ate foods I had never tried from the bulk bins at the Co-Op. I had the task of writing the numbers on a scrap of paper for the cashier. Dad's house was no-television quiet and he would often read lying on the couch, lit by the light coming in the bay windows. I had never known such long stretches of silence.

"What is it you were doing out there in the yard all morning?" he asked me once.

"Building an underground city."

He laughed. Proud, green eyes.

Many mornings we sat at The Spar Café, me coloring and watching the back and forth between Dad and whichever friend it was he talked and laughed with over steaming cups of coffee. We went to the library, carried our own groceries home from the store, spent many nice days at the beach where Dad did yoga on the sand, and I made castles decorated with kelp and any rocks or found objects I could scavenge.

I took recorder lessons in the park with Mac, an older man with a white beard who, though I did not know it then, was Dad's former lover, a lover who took him in when he was young, before he met Mom and tried going straight. I admired the way they leaned in and laughed together, how Mac's eyes smiled. I have always wondered at the details of their meeting, their falling in love, then back out of love, then into friendship. There were too many things I waited too long to ask Dad, worried if I pressed too hard he might leave. Once a parent leaves, even if they return, the fear remains. There will be time? Do not count on it. Those conversations, the really hard ones, can be avoided as long as you live. And the time is never right. I have wondered about a lot of things I have not had the courage to ask him.

Dad took me to Capitol Lake for lessons once a week all summer. For one half hour I would listen, then play, then listen, then play again, getting a little better each week, though I practiced only sporadically. When each lesson ended, I would play in the water at the edge of the lake and watch where Mac sat plump and cross-legged in baggy earth-toned clothing next to Dad who leaned back on his elbows, legs stretched out.

When the sun shone on Olympia, people came to the lake. I learned to play *Mary Had A Little Lamb* on the recorder sitting on a Mexican blanket among islands of blanket worlds. That was when the water was still safe to swim in. They would bring their picnics, their frisbees, and their floating lounge chairs. They brought their musty used copies of *Crime and Punishment* bought at Browser's Bookstore, their handwoven jewelry to sell. We walked most places we went. We did not own a car, and Dad did not like the bus, said it made him feel closed-in, eye-balled. For longer distances, even to friends who lived in more remote parts of town, we hitchhiked. Standing on the side of the road, the smell of dirt and exhaust, the surrounding spruce and alder trees, the open sky, I stuck out my thumb, hips askew. Dad said people were more likely to pick up a cutie-pie with pigtails and overalls than an old man. Our first time hitchhiking, Dad stuck his thumb out and watched some cars pass, to prove his point. I counted fifteen cars pass before he signaled for me to take over. When the very next car stopped, it was official.

I had the lucky thumb.

The rain started mid-September, then paused for a few weeks for an October Indian Summer, only to take the sun back seeming permanently afterward. A lid settled over town, leaving the lawn at the lake empty, the coffee shops full.

One of Dad's few female friends babysat me. Bev wrote children's books and loved women, not men. She had a pale, oval face that held a concerned expression. Thick-framed blue glasses shielded her narrow, dark eyes. Her thin, graying brown hair fell in a straight cut above her shoulders. She did not smile big or often, but she exuded wonder and confidence, took time to teach. Did you know that dogs sweat through the pads of their feet? That rainbows are created by mirrored light? That blue herons swallow their prey whole? She once gave me a signed copy of a book she wrote, signed *Love, Aunt Bev.*

The book is about a little girl who runs away from home and meets a woman in the city who owns a pretzel cart. The girl and the pretzel woman become friends, and the little girl takes a job helping her sell pretzels. The illustrations are in black and white. Within the drawings are all these tiny hidden pictures, like a butterfly in a pretzel and a giraffe under a man's top hat.

For a while, the girl's life is perfect. She never thinks of home. One spring day, though, Maria the pretzel woman meets Oscar and falls in love. Oscar owns a hot dog cart and loves Maria back.

In the falling in love drawing, there are hearts in their eyes and more, littler hearts coming off the tops of their heads. There is also a sailboat in Oscar's pocket and a motorcycle tucked in the pretzel woman's shoe. Their gazes are fixed on each other. The little girl is drawn standing in the far left corner of the page, alone, a pair of scissors where one braid should be.

I memorized all the hidden pictures there were to find. I wondered why the girl ran away in the first place, and why the story only showed the fence around her home as she left and then returned at the end of the book. Where were her parents?

After Dad met Jim, Bev babysat me at night. Though I tried to stay awake until Dad came home, even on nights I accomplished this, his eyes were far, far away and he would scold me, send me to bed. Had I been just a temporary distraction from his loneliness? A distraction he no longer needed?

Then, the breakfast I will never forget.

We ate at The Spar. Lu waited on us.

"Hey kiddo," she bumped her elbow against my shoulder.

"Hey, Lu. How are you?" We both laughed at the rhyme. We always did. A signature greeting exchanged since the first time it had popped out and Lu laughed so full she tossed her head back and stomped her foot.

I ordered the usual stack of pancakes, side of bacon, then pulled the tiny mason jar full of crayons closer, studied the new kids menu.

Waiting for our orders to arrive, sitting in the booth across from Dad and Jim, Dad told me. *You are going back to Aberdeen to live with your mother.* I asked *Why?* Thinking, *Was it me? Jim?*

Lu snuck our meals in, saying nothing.

Dad said didn't I know this was always temporary, hadn't he told me that? I shook my head *no*, tears on my cheeks, though we both knew I had. *When?* Today, he said. Jim looked at his watch, told me my bus would leave at 10:35, that I had plenty of time to finish my pancakes.

I cut the pancakes up into little bite-sized pieces, then left them there. Lu put them in a clamshell box that I purposely left behind, because I did not feel like eating pancakes, maybe not ever again.

Still crying after boarding the bus, waving a confused goodbye from the tiny, tinted window, I tucked the sack lunch Dad handed me for later into my bag.

Spinning, spinning, spinning.

I forgot to pack Bev's book. Years later, when I asked Dad about it, he only remembered there had been a book, but not where it went or what the title was. Every time I visit a used bookstore I browse the children's shelves, looking for it. I once searched the database at Powell's for every keyword I could think of and came up with nothing. I would love to read it again, see it again.

Huxley wrote that change is only possible through movement,

and Murakami wrote *I move therefore I am.*

The year I lived in Olympia the idea of movement settled in me, a tiny dormant seed.

THREE.

The day I descended the stairs of the Greyhound and walked into the frown that is downtown Aberdeen sticks in memory like a grass stain on denim. Downtown was already becoming ghostly, fifteen years before Walmart came to town. More bars than shops. More regulars in those bars than tourists passing through on their way to Westport or Ocean Shores. After that day I would live in Aberdeen for nearly a decade, but my heart would only ever be passing through.

I walked the long bus aisle to descend the steps, and there stood Mom, smiling radiantly, waiting for me to step off. I wore pigtails and a large gray backpack, carried the sack lunch I had not touched because I was not hungry and my stomach hurt. I had sat still the entire bus ride, eyes fixed out the window at the stream of tree after tree after tree. Nauseating.

The last time I had seen Mom, her eyes had pooled and run with tears and she had come back for three hugs before climbing into a car, driving away. When I stepped down the metal stairs onto the sidewalk, she again had tears in her eyes.

I froze, uncertain.

She scooped me up in her arms, lifted me off the ground and spun me around a few times, kissing me once on each cheek. I looked up to see her own round cheeks flushed and streaked, just before she put me down and wiped under her eyes with the outer edge of each index finger.

We describe love in terms of movement. I swooned, we say, or I was moved. Our palms sweat. Our mind races. We cannot breathe. Our hearts skip a beat. When we feel free, we move freely. As far as feeling goes, Mom has always been a wave crashing and receding, unceasing, unstoppable.

I could not see my features in her, not like I could in Dad, who had the same long forehead, same long fingers. Her hair was dark brown, but her face was round, not oval. Her blue eyes were globes, mine brown and almond-shaped. Short and flashy, she wore red lipstick and nail polish to match. She had warm soft skin and breath that smelled like cola. She looked different somehow, maybe happier.

"You've gotten so tall," she said, pressing me close. "Did you miss me?"

"Yes."

What else could I say?

I missed Dad.

Feeling a knot turn in my stomach, I opened my bag and peeked in the lunch sack: ham and cheese, an apple, a bag of chips, a Payday bar—a feast.

"It's okay if you didn't." She wiped her eyes, sniffling. "What kind of mother dumps her own daughter off like that?"

I did not respond, looking at my shoelaces, lifting my toes off the ground until I balanced on my heels.

"Well, come on. Let's get some pie." She pulled me toward her car. A bright yellow Beetle with a tie-dye colored cross hanging from the rear-view.

"I was supposed to work today," she said. "I got Alice to cover for me. It's your first night home, after all…"

"What about tomorrow? Who will watch me when you're at work? Will you have to quit your job?"

"Don't you worry, dear. I've got it covered." She giggled, bumped my chin with the flat of her knuckle.

We drove down a few streets and parked in a lot near one of the tallest buildings around. She pulled me through the swinging glass doors, beaming. I scanned the surroundings for clues of what to make of this place where the air hung thick with grease, smoke, and noise. We sat on stools at the counter in front of the kitchen, in clear view of the heat lamps and coffee pot, a spot I would come to know well.

The Smoke Shack was located on the bottom floor of a five-story building downtown. The owners rented the upper floors to low-income residents and earned a government kickback for doing so. The restaurant also housed a bar, a tobacco store, and a long counter for pull tabs and pool accessories: squares of blue chalk, cues with designer handles (some inlaid with pearl and coral, some with pearl and gold filler, some hand-carved) and also hats and T-shirts that read *Like My Rack?* and *Surgeon General's Warning: Bothering me about smoking may be hazardous to your health.*

Margaret, the gray-haired waitress with excess mascara and bleeding lipstick, kept saying she could not get over how adorable I was, pinching my cheeks and setting the biggest slice of coconut cream pie in front of me, playfully pressing her blue-lidded eye into a wink.

Joe, the cook, intimidatingly tall and strong, came out from the kitchen to get a peek, leaned in and gently tugged one of my pigtails.

"Well, aren't you the cutest thing? And have we heard about you!"

He patted my shoulder. "Boy does your mom love to brag on you, which means a lot because your mom is one helluva woman. But you know that, of course. Did you just get in?"

I could not make a reply; my eyes shifted to watch my feet dangling from the counter stool.

"Ah, you won't be shy for long," he said, patting my head and walking back into the kitchen. He put a steaming plate under the heat lamp, hit the bell with the palm of his hand, saluted me, then turned away.

He was right. I came to love sitting at that counter, spinning on my favorite stool, came to love telling Margaret what I had learned in school each day, hearing Joe brag about the special he had come up with for the night, came to love eating coconut cream pie and drinking weak coffee.

At home, we drank powdered milk and ate government cheese Mom picked up at the food bank, but she was always singing *even though we ain't got money* and I liked all the attention she gave me since it was just the two of us. Noah stayed with my Granny and Grampa, because Mom said Grampa could take him to baseball practice every day. At the time, this did not seem like a strange reason, though looking back, knowing how I feel about my daughters, I bet there must have been more to the story than that.

Fourth grade at McDermoth Elementary came easy to me, even though I had missed the entire previous year. Mom would drop me at the morning play care so she could make her early morning class, then she would pick me up every day at 3:03.

Our teacher, Ms. Wright, wore her white-gray hair piled on top of her head, and the chalk clicked as she filled the entire board with sentences for us to copy and math problems to solve.

"Why weren't you in school before?" The girl who sat behind me (Miranda) asked one day.

"I don't know," I said. "My dad homeschooled me."

For reading and writing, we worked at our own pace through different colored booklets, a different cartoony animal mascot for each one. When I finished a booklet, I earned an item from the prize table. The prizes were not all that great. A paddleball, *Great Job!* stickers, and a ceramic squirrel are three of the treasures I brought home. Of course I liked getting prizes, but mostly I liked being good at something. I wanted our teacher to run out of booklets for me to read.

I excelled at spelling, blowing bubbles, and doing cartwheels. Mom would tug my hair into two French braids that reached below my shoulder blades, pull the hair so taut it hurt.

"Ouch," I would say.

"You look beautiful," she would reply, looking at me with her *don't-you-know-how-special-you-are* mother eyes.

Mom made clothes from Butterick patterns. Culottes. Ruffles. Bell-bottom polyester pants in beige, with matching beige vest. Shoulder-tie blouses. Busy prints.

Left to my own inclination? Jeans, plain colored t-shirts, and tennis shoes. Mom dressed me up in her strange creations and left a trail of photographic evidence. Close-ups with various cheesy grins, different teeth missing in each one. Action photos where I might be running away from the camera and maybe you just see the cut of a velour vest, the flash of a ruffled, yellow sleeve.

Mom talked to strangers, and strangers wanted to share their most intimate secrets with her. She did not seem to have that same sense of what kinds of things a person should not talk about in public, to strangers. "When my mom had her first mental breakdown...", she would say or "I had the worst diarrhea," when others might say, "my mom was ill when I was a child" or "it didn't settle well with me." She remembered names, pets' names, and she especially remembered all the stories people told her about who had died or might die, who had cheated, and who was addicted to drugs or had landed his or her ass in prison. Mom embarrassed me when she talked too much to perfect strangers about our lives, so I clammed up. "She's a little shy," Mom would explain, the hint of concern in her voice that certain parents have.

I had mild asthma compared to my brother, who had to take "treatments" from a machine that burbled, emitted a smoke-like vapor that smelled of burning wires and left a bitter taste on the tongue. I had a rasp that got worse in the spring, and even worse when I was feeling especially shy. Once I sat waiting for my turn to stand up and recite "The Charge of the Light Brigade" to the class and by the time my name was called my breath had reduced to a rattling wheeze. Mom took me to the hospital where the nurse said I needed a shot. I panicked and refused to let anyone touch me.

"Well, you aren't so shy now," mom said, helping one nurse hold me down while another gave the injection.

Mom had a voice that gave you goose bumps and she used it all day. Whenever she felt the desire: humming or saying *hey, do you know how that song that goes...?*

She leaned a lot on me then. *What should I do?* She would ask.

What should I wear? Can you help me stick to this diet? Do you think there's something wrong with me? She called me strong and told me how proud she was to have a strong, smart daughter. I believed her, which made for a pretty serious fourth grader. *You're so wise*, she would say.

A mega-nerd with hayfever sniffles, I got pushed in the hall and teased that I had cooties or lice or ringworm, something only the gross kids had. The kids who ate free lunch and wore knock-off Keds and discount designer jeans. The shy kids, the slow kids, the poor kids, the ones who got caught picking their noses in class.

But this was the year I met Mindy and we started writing our superhero comic, *The Wacky Fruit Gang*. So, at least, I had a way to fight off evil.

Jeff Jenkins, for instance. He tripped me in the hall every day, pulled my braids, and called me nerd, his finger pressed to the tip of his nose to make a face like a pig.

One October afternoon, I walked home, kicking piles of leaves as I went. Mindy and I usually walked together, but she stayed home sick that day. When my legs flew out from under me and I fell face-first onto the pavement, I had been looking up at the fat white clouds, thinking the sky looked strangely blue. I knew right away who to blame for my bleeding and scraped palms and knees, his laugh high and mean like no other laugh I have heard since. Reason gone, I charged at him, screaming *you stupid motherfucker I'm going to kill you* (vocabulary I had picked up sitting on a bar stool at The Smoke Shack waiting for Mom's shift to end). He ran! He outran me, yes, and I fell in a hole and twisted my ankle so hard I had to wear a cast for six weeks. But, he ran. That is what mattered.

Mom believed me when I told her I had been running home to catch the conclusion of the after school special and that I was looking at the sky, not the sidewalk in front of me, and it was sort of true. She felt so sorry for me she stopped at Baskin Robbins after we left the emergency room and let me order a double-scoop of peppermint ice cream.

I pulled rocks out of my knee for months after that day, even after it healed and new skin had grown over. Sometimes a hot bath would draw a rock out, which seemed a bit like magic every time it happened.

We did laundry on Sundays after church and shopped for groceries, too. I loved holding the hand-sewn red velvet bag we kept the laundry quarters in, switching out the loads when they were done, learning to fold.

At the grocery store, we played the coupon game. Mom would

give me a stack of coupons and send me with my own cart to locate the items on the coupons, direct me to match the brand and size, to gather the quantity she had written in the corner. I loved hearing how much I saved us with my coupons, waited anxiously for her to add it up.

After a while, she let me take over the coupons altogether, saying I was much better at it than she was. She watched the laundry turning round and round in the big machines, reading a magazine, and I would take a stack of coupons and a cart to do the shopping.

"I'll be over to pay in a half hour", she would say. "Good luck."

Usually I would still be in the aisles carefully studying a coupon for product type and limit or studying a box of cereal or can of soup, keeping time on my pink Timex when Mom arrived with her wallet. If she had not shown and I had finished, I would park my cart over by the front doors and run over to get her. She would say, "Done already? You're getting too fast for me!"

Because Mom was working full-time and taking night classes at the community college, our neighbor, Mary, babysat me for free. When I came home from school and Mom had not made it home from class, I went straight to Mary's. When Mom worked graveyard, I stayed home alone under the instruction that *should I need anything, anything at all*, I was to go to Mary's. Should I find Mary's door locked, I could find the key in the very bottom of the mailbox. She had me practice retrieving it: I could reach it out of the white metal lidded box to the right of the front door, but I had to stand on tiptoes to reach all the way to the bottom.

White-haired Mary rarely left the sanctuary of her wing-backed burnt-orange armchair and watched television all day and into the night, her eyes opening and closing at intervals. Mom shopped for her, washed her dishes and laundry, and put fresh sheets on her bed.

An avocado plant towered over Mary's chair. I had never seen a plant so tall or so boldly green, with long, oval leaves.

"What kind of plant is that?" I asked.

She told me it was an avocado plant that she had grown herself.

"How did you grow it?" I asked.

Instead of answering she told me to bring an avocado and a handful of toothpicks the next day. Mom indulged me when I asked if we could go to the store and buy one. As I look back on it, she must have been impressed that I had wanted an avocado, and not the usual pack of gum or candy bar. After school the next day, I went straight to Mary's with the fruit I had tucked into my book bag that morning. Mary and I ate the avocado together. She sliced it in half and removed the pit, setting it aside. Then, she took a jar of mayonnaise from the refrigerator and filled the pit-hole with a spoonful of mayo. We each had one half. She showed me how to fill jelly jars with water and place toothpicks in the pit and explained that, most of all, they just needed sunlight and time. *Avocados*, she said, *are good for your heart.*

To this day, when I see an avocado pit sunning in a kitchen window, I am standing in Mary's dusty apartment looking for evidence of friends, long-lost children, a dead husband. Any indication that she is not as lonely as she seems, that that kind of loneliness could not happen to a person like her or me.

Mom and I made rare and strange visits to her mom, always with the weight of the question *Is she on her meds?* I had picked up pieces of stories of what we might find if she was not. I knew she had been arrested downtown, wearing just her bra and underwear, yelling something which no one wanted to repeat. *She gets crazy when she's not on her meds,* Mom said. *She imagines things.*

I worried what she might imagine about me, so watchful and worried. But her blue eyes smiled, and she listened when I talked as if whatever I said was secret-important.

One night, Mom said we needed to go check on Grandma. I could tell something was wrong by the creases on Mom's brow, by the way she chewed her nails. We drove across town to Grandma's third-story apartment and walked around back. One mismatched shoe sat on each step, up two narrow flights of stairs, placed as if they were walking to the door, where a painted sign hung on it read, "Jesus Saves."

Mom heaved a heavy sigh, then knocked.

"Oh, it's you!" Grandma said, as if she had been expecting us. She talked and talked and I could not follow what she said.

"Want some macaroni?" she asked. "It's homemade."

I nodded. She served me a bowl of the cheesiest, creamiest macaroni I have ever tasted. Mom asked her when she had last taken her meds. The question bothered her, as she paced the floor. She insisted that her doctors were crazy, that she did not need medication, that it had made her sick. Then, abruptly, she asked, "Did you hear them when you came up the stairs?"

We sat on a deep brown sofa that sunk in when you sat on it, so I could not put my feet on the ground. I wondered for a flash if I might get lost in it, sinking there. Mom and Grandma talked while Grandma smoked, and Grandma kept pinning me with her tender light-blue eyes, "Do you want some macaroni, dear? I made homemade." "No, thank you," I kept saying, eyes looking everywhere but at her, except for a second to shyly smile. Didn't she remember I had two bowls already?

I had the impression my smile delighted her, and I guessed she lacked moments of delight. Maybe it was the shoes scattering the floor or the collection of dolls with rosy cheeks and eyes that rolled back. Maybe it was the way she jumped up to count her spoons or the smell of custard in the air. As often as she regarded me with a smile (nearly every time she ever looked at me), the impression her smile gave was that she made a conscious effort, a battle against the chaos in her head, to give me that smile.

The rain came hard in October and the sky seemed darker earlier than before. The wind whipped the leaves into eddies, rang the wind-chimes and left us without power for two whole days. Walking home from school in the near dark after dropping Mindy at her house, I imagined people hiding behind trees, the sound of footsteps following close behind. Though I tried to reason with my imagination, I ended up running home, slamming the door closed behind me, feeling I'd had another close call, struggling to catch my breath.

Spinning, spinning, spinning.

I began writing to escape my real life. Mindy and I created a comic book filled with fruit superheroes and vegetable villains. The crazier the adventure, the better. Crazy Carrot, the villain of all villains, jealous because fruits are just more likable, schemed to destroy The Wacky Fruit Gang (led by Artie Apple and Ollie Orange, our alter egos).

Lying on our bellies on the carpet, Mindy and I sketched and wrote captions, sometimes for hours at a time. Finding out what a kumquat looked like constituted a minor quest that involved getting a ride to the library, where we researched and made lists of different fruits and vegetables.

Crazy Carrot tried to take over the world. He tried poisoning the Wacky Fruit Gang and stealing all of their shoes. He could never win because he had no heart. He tried and tried, but he always ended up flat on his ass, just like Tom the Cat and Wile E. Coyote.

Our plots were simple and too easily resolved, but we did not know that then. We were just learning how to move through a story. We most enjoyed making up the characters, drawing them out and filling in each character page with personality traits, and favorite foods, and all the details we could think of to bring that character to life. It would be years before I would read, head-nodding, Woolf's spider's web simile, but even then I had a sense of how moving through stories might move me too, and hopefully others. And I craved that journey.

I wrote my own work secretly. Mostly poetry, full of concept words, not images, typical of a beginner. It is really the concepts that compel us to write: hypocrisy, beauty, pain. It takes practice to learn how to communicate them artfully, and desire. Loads of desire. I began to carry a notebook with me everywhere I went, sometimes two or three. And I suppose those notebooks were the first draft of this story.

And why write this story, so vulnerable and so mine? Because we seem obsessed with stories of frailty, and I want to contribute a different verse. Dylan Thomas wrote *the force that drives the water through the rocks drives my red blood* and I swooned when I read that line, because he knew what I knew. Pen in hand, ink filling page after page after page. Typewriter drum moving right—left—right—left. Cursor following the words as they fill screen after screen. Writing could change my mind, spring my tears, show me what I really thought. The more I wrote, the more I became. Without writing I stood still, unable to speak or move, just like in the recurring dream that has played in my sleep since I was a little girl.

I am standing in an alley, blackberry bushes grown out of control. I am stomping on bushes to get through the alley, trying not to catch my clothing on the thorns.

A man approaches. One look at him and I know he wants to hurt me.

His eyes are dark pools.

He is not smiling.

I try to scream and nothing comes out.

I try to run and I find my feet cemented to the ground.

Wide-mouthed silent scream.

I wake in a sweat, terrified.

FOUR.

Mom was stretched thin, for sure. But the best time I remember spending with her falls into the space between coming to live with her and my meeting Ray. I must have been aware they were dating, but it was not until his black Chevy van pulled up to our house one summer day that he even registered with me as really existing at all. Black hair to his shoulders, feathered out in that Shaun Cassidy way. His wide smile revealed a tooth black at the tip, rimmed with gold. He said *aren't you the cutest girl* and pinched my arm so it hurt a little.

"Show her your van," Mom said. We stood on the sidewalk outside our apartment. The setting sun left a reluctant smear of purple and red across the sky.

"Wait. Turn on the stereo first. So she can get the full effect." Mom's attention, a beam of light, focused on Ray. He swaggered to the driver side on platform heels, bell bottoms swaying, opened the door, and did what needed to be done to get disco music pumping. He came back around to the other side of the van, sucked his teeth, opened the double doors to reveal big black speakers, fully red-carpeted interior with a bed and a TV in the back.

Ray started showing up every evening. He played guitar and sometimes we would sing along to Keith Green or Dylan. Sometimes we would eat dinner and then I would watch TV while Mom and Ray sat in the kitchen talking. Sometimes we watched movie marathons like Bruce Lee or Shirley Temple Week. A few times we played Parcheesi.

I got used to Ray's trying-too-hard smile and the way he pinched me and sucked his teeth. I liked the way he pulled me close and sang the refrain *beautiful girl, beautiful girl*, a song he said he had written for me.

I was nine, turning ten in winter when Ray moved in. Noah moved back too, for what Mom said was a trial, to see how it would go. He wanted to stay with our Granny and Grampa, *but damn it*, she said, *he's my son, he should be here with us. I shouldn't be saying this to you*, she added, but kept talking anyway about how they had not meant to but they had taken away her firstborn, her only son.

I wish I could say that Ray did not fool me, but he did. He showered me with the attention I craved, bought me ice cream, talked

Mom into letting me stay up late, and composed spontaneous little songs about my smile and the way I picked flowers.

It has been years since I could even admit there was a time I liked him, a time, even, when I too (in a sense) had fallen in love with him. For the sake of the story I have to tell the truth here. As much as I wish I had been a stronger Eve, a wiser Eve. I was not.

I wanted Ray to move in. I have seen it in a few photos that I can now barely stand to look at. Before long (and at Mom's urging) I began trying out the title *Daddy*. He doted, even letting me sit on his lap when Mom and he talked close-together. He let me crawl into bed with them on nights I got scared, called me his little angel.

We moved into a house with a good-sized front and back yard for turning cartwheels, a swing in back, pale yellow and red rhododendron bushes on either side of a wood-planked porch I liked to pretend to tap-dance on. Noah, now twelve, possessed limbs that could morph into his weapon of choice on the whim of his imagination. Only extreme boredom could bring him to play with me, and even then he insisted on bringing his guns and swords.

The initial excitement of the place faded once we had all moved in, once Mom started night-shift work at the hospital cleaning sick people and administering their medications, once Ray started coming into my room at night.

I stumbled into the age of secrets, and the secrets were more and more. Too many.

Spinning, spinning, spinning.

In this time of secrets, I was not supposed to tell about walking in on my older brother smoking, eyes blood-shot from crying.

"What's wrong?" I asked.

"None of your business. And don't you dare fucking tell!"

Closed door.

I was not supposed to tell about the candy bars Mom hid away. I was not supposed to tell the secrets about boys my girlfriends began offering me in whispers and notes passed. Every secret carried with it a weight that left me a little more silent. It seemed my friendships hinged on one thing now: *Can you keep a secret?* I especially was not supposed to tell about how, in the black of midnight, Ray snuck into my room, sucking his teeth, about how the sound of his breath, full of desire, squeezed my secret heart.

"She's so nice, such a quiet, serious girl," my fourth grade teacher remarked at a parent-teacher conference.

"Yes, she's a very bright girl," Mom answered. "Her brother is bright, too. I'm so proud."

Quiet and *serious* did not resonate with the person I wanted to be.

Despite—perhaps encouraged by—comments from family on how I had been such a motor mouth before, I went inward. In the way flowing water will find an easy path, I found that silent contemplation was a place without secrets. I began to put everything down on paper, to fill notebook after notebook with anything my heart desired, what I could not utter aloud.

From the outside, we made a happy family. We went to church together every Sunday, ate dinner together every night. Mom ran Bible studies for the ladies at the church and made Ray's favorite dishes. Ray worked swing shift as a janitor and she worked graveyard at the community hospital. For the first time in our lives, we were not renting the house we lived in. We owned. Mom bought a white Mercedes. Used, but a Mercedes, nonetheless.

The yellow house sat at the end of a street that crossed two main drags and cut a line through the entire Westside of Aberdeen. We lived at the dead end. I spent most of my time on the front lawn or in my room. I did cartwheels and waited to see who might emerge from one of the neighboring houses. In back, the yard pushed right up against a hill and some woods that seemed to lead to nowhere. I know because I tried climbing that steep hill again and again and never got past the shrubs and trees. There was a flat ridge that made a nice picnic spot with a secret view of the neighbor's backyards. In my room, I read, wrote in my journal or, until I grew out of them, composed dramatic stories between my Strawberry Shortcake dolls.

In truth, Ray held our household underwater. He raged unpredictably. Sometimes I talked back, and he would laugh or comment on what a clever girl I was. Other times his eyes would flash to black, and I would not know the direction his anger would take. *Had I said something? Was it Mom? Noah?* In a way, I preferred it when I was the focus because then I had some role in the drama of yelling, throwing things, belt or hand on flesh that would unfold, some measurable thing I was being punished for. When Noah and Mom were the punished ones, I could only watch and listen, and in my own way (usually in my head) try to defend, emitting *don'ts* and *waits*, trying to prevent Ray from becoming the tsunami of anger that would engulf our house, leave us all spent of breath or explanation.

Ray punched Noah for getting a D in English and for playing Dungeons and Dragons, "the devil's work." He threw a vase at Mom for having her own opinion and for being nosy. Talking back is mostly what could prompt him to take off his belt and lash out at me.

One Fourth of July sticks in memory, one of those images that pool and collect to make up who you are, what you struggle with. One of the memories that precipitated the telling of this story, this taking of inventory, this tale of how movement can unstick us from woe.

Noah and his friends were on the front lawn lighting firecrackers under slugs, then running away. The sky was just going dark, and the air smelled of gunpowder and barbecue. I had spilled a soda earlier that left my hands sticky.

"Eve!" Ray called me inside.

I did not budge from my spot by the camellia bush where I stood collecting blossoms in a bowl of water. I heard my name again and again.

When he came out and grabbed me by the hair I did not have to look at his eyes to know that what came next would hurt, would last. He dragged me up the wooden stairs to the upper floor where our bedrooms were, but I would not go lightly.

"I hate you!" I screamed and kicked and struggled to get free.

Calling me disrespectful with a hiss and a tug, he dragged me to my room. The hairdryer that I had used that morning trying to style my noncompliant hair sat on the floor, still plugged into the wall. I expected him to take off his belt, like usual. Instead, he tore the plug from the socket and cursed as he hit me again and again. *Ungrateful. Disrespectful. Unlady-like. Stupid, stupid girl.*

I fell asleep to the boom of fireworks out my window, counting welts.

A few weeks later, Mom and I spent a weekend alone. Ray went fishing with friends, and Noah was spending most weekends at our Granny and Grampa's. We rented *Cocoon* and Mom made buttery popcorn and cinnamon hot chocolate. We sat together on the couch, my head resting on her shoulder, her combing my hair with her fingers.

"I'm sorry," she said.

"What for?" I asked.

"For being weak. For not standing up for you."

"You don't stand up for yourself, either," I said.

"I know. I should. I really should."

That was the end of the conversation, but I thought we had reached an agreement, that *I'm sorry* meant I will do different in the future, you do not have to worry anymore. At the time, I felt betrayed when nothing changed the way I thought it would.

I did not know then what I know now about movement. About how big change occurs. I did not know then how sometimes the very feelings that cause us to desire a change are the same feelings that keep us following the same patterns as before.

One morning, all smiles and kisses, Mom pulled me out of school early to take me shopping because, she said, my pants were all high-waters.

"You're growing like a weed."

"Do I have to try them on?" I whined.

In the dressing room, I snapped the waist button closed. I could hear Mom's breathing on the other side of the door, then she said something I did not catch.

"What?" I asked.

"We're getting married. This summer. You're going to be a flower girl."

Stunned silence.

"Let me see how the pants look," she said.

I stepped out. She spun my stiff body around to see both sides, tugged on the pockets and waistband, inspected the seams.

"These pants look great on you. Isn't that exciting? How you're going to be my flower girl?"

"Yes." My ability to lie flourished as the secrets grew, as I understood it did not matter how I really felt about anything. Telling the truth hurt feelings, landed me in hot water, created conflict.

That night, I tried to run one hundred circles around the house. Mom and Ray thought it was strange, but harmless, even admirable, because it showed such determination. Why did I do it? I could not tell you the reason. It was a compulsion to run until I felt out of breath, my heart thumping like I might float away or die on the spot. Because I did not float away or die, I felt strong and capable, which was a new and wonderful feeling. Is that when the seed became a sprout? I cannot be sure the precise cause and effect, which is why I am telling this story in pieces. What I do know is that we are all of us capable of being that girl in the alley near the blackberry bushes and we are all of us capable of moving through the alley.

Our bodies have a lot to do with that.

As promised, Mom married her teeth-sucking nighthawk in a small ceremony at the church we now attended every Sunday. I squirmed in the ruffled pink dress Mom made and the black strappy flats she insisted I wear. I could not seem to rearrange my nylon tights so they would not itch, no matter how I adjusted the crotch and seams. A bouquet of red poppies and white daisies in hand, I stood next to them.

When they kissed, I noticed Mom's eyes, closed, thin, and pale.

Noah sat sulking next to the pastor's son, but no one paid him any mind. Adolescents are expected to sulk. He sulked right through Mom's rendition of "Flesh of My Flesh." *You are flesh of my flesh, bone of my bone. We are one.* That is what I remember. Noah sulking, uncomfortable clothes, adults singing and talking, and a sense of spinning, spinning, spinning. I thought I might pass out, or words would pop out of my mouth without my meaning to. So I pinched my lips together, bit the inside of my cheek. I tried to focus on one thing at a time. I studied the hymnal in front of me, a coverless hardback, linen to the touch, a faded antique green, gold-embossed lettering. I reached for it and turned it over in my hands. The pages crisp, thin, and gold-edged. I pretended to read the musical notes above the words. On the back of the hymnal, *Grace Assembly Church* and *Aberdeen, WA* stamped in bleeding black ink. I put it back and focused on the woman in front of me, the way her head tipped to the left. I examined every stained-glass window, the dark colors where no light came through, the faces seeming scared, except for the absent-eyed angels flying by.

Then the wedding got churchy, revival churchy. The music started and people were swaying in the aisles, speaking in tongues and yelling *Hallelujah, glory be to God.* I endured by looking hard at one thing, then the next, letting each object take my mind someplace else.

After the ceremony, there was a potluck in the basement. I filled my entire plate with sweet "salads," thinking how Mom would tell me to eat my protein first. Three colors of jello and a fruit salad too. For seconds, I ate barbecue chips. I ate until my stomach ached, then I went out to the gravel parking lot to throw rocks at the thin metal door of the would-be garage, now church storage shed. When Mom found me she screeched, "What are you doin' girl?" the same way she did when I absent-mindedly cut the arm of the couch to shreds with a pair of scissors. She pulled me toward her by one arm, dusted the dirt off my dress with determined slaps of her open palm.

Now an official stepdad, Ray's bragging about me increased, as if he held more claim to me now. He carried on as if he were my flesh and blood father, about my smarts, my beauty, my obedience. When people commented on how shy I was, he gave me a shoulder hug of approval. He doted and enforced his strict rules. I could not spend the night at other people's houses, ride a bike (unlady-like), or listen to secular music.

When Ray's temper flared, the whole house cowered. The lash of his belt. The force of his hand on the back of a head. His clenching of the soft space between neck and shoulder. The way his eyes darkened in an instant, his spirit turned. Mom, Noah, and I learned to recognize triggers and avoid them as best we could, which sometimes was as impossible as avoiding spelling tests or school bullies.

Mom could not say yes to anything without asking what Ray thought first. Sometimes he got pissed just because she asked. She cooked his favorite foods and dished up his plate. She stopped singing all the time and started randomly hugging me and saying *you know I love you, right?*

The rains fell hard that September and my umbrella kept blowing inside out. The Hills neighborhood rose a couple of miles east of the flatlands that made up the westside neighborhood where I lived. Rich kids live in the Hills who, until middle school, would be only the mysterious visiting sports teams from across town: elusive, unreal, and most importantly, impotent, therefore incapable of affecting our social status the way they would when we were all dumped into high school together.

Sequestered in our apartments and modest homes, we Westsiders hung together in order to keep from sliding into the puddles of our sinking lawns, puddles that devoured whole sections of the streets where we played, riding our bikes from ditch to ditch. Among the sprawling, unmanageable blackberry bushes, we congregated, collected tadpoles, formed clubs, shared secrets, eventually held hands and smoked cigarettes that came from the same store where we once bought penny candy.

Our family crossed town to get to Grace Assembly Pentecostal Church. Twice on Sunday and once on Wednesday night, we attended services. Beyond that, special events like Harvest celebrations (in lieu of Halloween), holiday services, and Christian Eagle meetings brought us back to the church nearly every day. Church leaders spent heaps of effort to make God appealing to us children, doling out prizes for memorizing bible verses and sending us on camping retreats.

There was no getting out of the weekly drives to church. We would park in the loose gravel parking lot and ascend the wide, tall, wood staircase to the house of God with its vaulted ceilings and columns of dark, hardwood pews. I would sit with Mom, waiting for service to start, watching the familiar faces, pretending to read the hymnal, but really just hiding. I would feel the crinkle of its thin pages, the sturdiness of its spine. I tried to place myself in the preacher's heavy words, tried so desperately sometimes that I put words to my effort, claimed I wanted Jesus in my heart. I had convinced myself of other things just by saying they were so before. Why not this too?

One Sunday at a revival, the preacher called for sinners to volunteer themselves, to come up to the altar and kneel for forgiveness. When I stood and pushed my way out of the pews and up the aisle, I heard approval uttered all around me. *Hallelujah*, they said, *Praise the Lord for this child*. I knelt at the altar. One woman flooded my crouched body with tongue-words that scared me.

I said exactly what she coaxed me to.

Jesus forgive me my sins. Come into my heart so that I might sin no more.
As I tell this now, I think of how—years later—I saw the woman who
swore so many Hallelujahs for my salvation picking up her mail at the
post office. Though I had heard her oldest son committed suicide a few
years after that revival, I offered no words to her. I saw her and looked
away, pretending not to know her.

Will I be forgiven for that sin, too?

I came to the altar willingly, asked Jesus into my life, made Mom
proud. I wanted to remain in the fold. But I just could not get past the
fact that while my congregation cheered and clapped for Mom and Ray
who played guitar and sang devotionals on stage, I knew better. Flesh
tempted them both. I memorized Bible verses, sold candy bars for Jesus,
and wrote a letter to the school superintendent protesting the teaching
of evolution in our class. Mom helped me with the ideas, I crafted the
words.

I did try.

Noah broke four windows tossing his baseball at the couch. He
spent most weekends at Granny and Grampa's house and even when he
was home he was not home, always out with his friends or at baseball
practice.

I envied him. The rules differed for me.

Three more years (ten-eleven-twelve): two spelling bee championships, my first kiss (a peck inside a giant tire in the middle of the school playground), and chicken pox, among other things too sweet and sour to remember now. Sometimes during those years, I convinced myself that Ray was not all that bad, that we were all okay. Mostly though, I dreamed I might be saved, and that my prince would be handsome, brave, and smart like Noah. Someday, I dreamed, when I was older. I did not know then that was just the kind of thinking that would prove to be the most significant impediment to my survival, in the soul sense. I did not know movement would save me. My own movement. Practiced movement.

The afternoon I gave up Jesus, I rode my bike to the Honda pits for some cardboard sliding. After rummaging through the garage to find the perfect-sized piece of cardboard for sliding down the dirt hills of summer, I trudged up the tallest hill to slide down, then up again, all the time trying to come to what I really believed. Accepting Jesus into my heart had not delivered me from suffering, had not made my smile match the zealots in our congregation. Little had changed when I attempted the devoted life. Mom bragged about me a little more, but I did not even want that. Mind full of questions, something in the sliding pulled me where I needed to go, loosened a mental knot or two. I knew that once

I had climbed the tallest hill, settled onto my piece of cardboard and kicked off, there would be that point when my breath caught in joyous fear, and I would get that calm after the adrenaline release. It happened that way so many times I lost count. Then I walked home exhausted, dirt-covered, a rebellious secret all my own.

FIVE.

One foggy morning, Mom woke me without the usual calamity of noise, cheer, and ultimatums. Though the threats never had the effect she hoped they would, it was always *Come On And Wake Up Now* in a sing-song voice or *I'm going to dump a glass of water over your head.* The morning I am remembering now, she sat on the edge of the bed and gently shook me. Out my window, I could see why I had struggled all night to stay warm, why my toes tingled cold.

The bright leaves of fall, frozen, would drift to the ground in short time, leaving the trees bare. Cold enough for hats and gloves now, you had to sit in the car to warm it up in the mornings, and could see your breath while you waited, shivering.

"Wake up, Eve. I've got a surprise for you."

I rolled over, stretched my legs, and moaned.

She shook me again. "Come on honey. Wake up."

"What is it?" I asked.

"I'm taking you to breakfast."

"I have to go to school."

"Not today you don't."

This woke me.

"Why did you let me take the day off to go out to breakfast?" I asked on the walk from the car to the waiting area of the restaurant. I was not sure I wanted to know. I kept fumbling with the cassette tapes in the console, putting on one, then popping it out and trying another. I opened the glove box and searched its contents. Mom filled what would have been silence with small talk about the church fundraiser, a patient of hers at work, and her opinion on the race for president.

"I just thought it would be a nice thing to do together." Definitely not the whole story.

A woman wearing a brown smock, her hair tied up in a yellow ribbon, seated us, took our drink order, and placed two glossy menus on the table.

When she returned, we both ordered Grand Slams. Mom chose bacon; I chose sausage. She took her eggs sunny-side up; I had mine scrambled. I stared out the window, watching the frozen cars pass, the jacketed and scarved people shivering down the sidewalk. I used five packs of sugar in my coffee, four creams, but I felt awfully grown up holding the heavy stoneware mug aloft with two fingers of my right hand. Breakfast on a school day? Just the two of us? She encouraging me to order coffee?

"What's new with you, honey? How's school?"

Pause. "Fine."

" I wish you would be more forthcoming."

"I'm not sure what you mean."

"I wish you'd share more with me."

"There's nothing to share."

She sighed.

"You have something to share, though, don't you?" I sipped my coffee, took a bite of buttery toast.

"Yes," she said. "I do."

I looked out the window.

"You're going to have a little sister," she said.

A sister could be good, I thought in the silence of the news.

Maybe Ray would not get angry with a baby around. Maybe with a daughter all his own to focus on he would forget about me, only he would not sneak into her room because she would be his real daughter.

"That's great," I said, moving the scraps of food around on my plate, shifting my feet back and forth under the table.

"You don't sound very excited," Mom's face drooped.

"When will she be born?"

"May. May first if she's on time."

"Will I have to share a room with her?"

"She'll be too little at first. By the time she's old enough, we plan to expand the house by two bedrooms at least. Ray is already working on the permits."

"What will you name her?"

"We haven't decided that yet."

"You should name her Meg, like Meg from *A Wrinkle In Time*."

"I'll put that suggestion on my list." She smiled.

After breakfast, Mom drove me to school, and that afternoon we had an assembly on peer pressure, then a test in math. I fell silent, and my friends kept asking me what was wrong and was I feeling okay and

I kept saying *yes, yes, I'm fine.* Jennifer-snooty-face who was perfect and perfectly bossy told me that if I wanted to play hopscotch with them at recess I needed to turn my frown upside down, so I quit and played with the younger kids on the parallel bars.

Life improved with Mom pregnant. Ray did not get angry as often, and never hit Mom. There were doctor check-ups and Lamaze classes, and best of all—a baby shower with cake, ruffle chips, and lemon-lime soda. I was old enough to be included with the other women in the games, and when Mom opened gifts I wrote down the names and a short description of the gift given: three onesies, hooded polka-dot bath towel, *Goodnight Moon.*

Then, on a Tuesday in early May, a note came from the office during Art. We were making mosaic self-portraits out of magazine clippings and tissue paper. The bright pink note said: *Your grandparents will pick you up out front after school.* When the bell rang and I had gathered up my backpack and yellow lunchbox, I walked out the front doors to find their station wagon idling at the curb and I climbed in the back with Noah. Granny sat on the passenger side and turned round to greet me while Grampa searched for a chance to pull out, took a deep drag of his Pall Mall and then hung his smoking arm out the window. "Your mom's at the hospital," Granny said. "Her water broke. You'll stay with us tonight and wait for the good news."

Granny made potatoes au gratin with little bits of ham and garlic green beans, and the four of us played Rummy until way past bedtime. I could wait up as late as I wanted and I did not have to go to school the next day. Noah beat me at rummy three times and Grampa chain smoked and made jokes the entire time while Granny waited for the phone to ring, filling in her nightly crossword puzzle. During the last hand of Rummy we played, I had trouble keeping my eyes open while waiting for Noah and Grampa to take their turns. I could feel the weight of my head nodding toward the table, so I put ice in my water and asked a lot of questions to keep myself awake. I had dozed off in Grampa's green recliner by the time the call came. There is a photo of me in that moment. Light blue pajama nightgown, tired eyes, messy long hair, phone receiver to my ear, getting the news that I had a baby sister named Carmen. She had dark eyes and dark hair and was now asleep in Mom's arms.

Having a sister was mostly good. I liked the sound of her coo and how she curled her toes when you touched the soft skin on the bottom of her feet. But her arrival also meant more chores for me. Mom and Ray expected me to "help with the baby," even change diapers. They expected me to babysit, and too often I was called into the room to see the next great performance. *Oh, look! She is singing along with the commercial! Oh, look! She will be crawling in no time!*

Noah spent weekends at our grandparents' (as always) and during the week, Grampa carted him from practice to practice. We often did not see him until dinnertime.

"He's so private." Mom tried to explain why he spent most of his time in his room or out with his friends. Is it privacy that drew me to him, made me want to be closer to him? Who knows, but I would have followed him to join the circus had he asked. I read the books on the lists he gave me, like *The Hobbit* and *The Chronicles of Narnia*. I started collecting baseball cards like he did. I even tried playing baseball, and learned the term "space cadet" when a baseball I was supposed to catch whacked me in the forehead during a game. I did not even make it through my first season before I quit.

Ray's temper did not disappear, and now we had a baby to worry about. It is bad enough living with someone who might explode at any moment, but having a tiny sister who cries and constantly needs feeding and changing made it harder to keep the house calm and free from danger. Mom would pick Carmen up when Ray got mad at me or Noah, holding her close to her chest, burying Carmen's face into her bosom. When Mom had upset him she would tell me to take my sister and go to my room and stay there.

A year passed and Carmen toddled toward stardom. Nothing I did made her hate me, though I sometimes tried because it was hard enough to protect myself here, and I did not want the burden of a sister. I would not let her play with my dolls, even though I had not played with them myself in years, and sometimes I hid hers. I turned the channel from her favorite TV shows and covered her mouth so she could not babble when she wanted to. Then I would feel bad, and I would give her an airplane or a piggy-back ride. I would read the same book to her over and over. I pulled her close. I pushed her away.

Running underneath all this was the knowledge that sometimes the tiniest thing, a tone, a gesture, an innocent deed, could be the flare that lit the fuse that would blow the whole scene up. You could not avoid an explosion forever, and sometimes all it took was a dirty dish or an unwanted question.

Avoidance of any kind of trouble took possession of me. I was uncomfortable when others talked in class, back-talked teachers or cheated on their work. I read directions carefully and followed them. I answered every bonus question, ticked off finished math packets and always traded my library books for more.

I was getting accustomed to our volatile life, even mastering it. Or so I thought, until finally my baby sister was the target of the blast. Carmen, two years old, with a thick snot cold, refusing to take her medicine. Ray shook her, tried to push the medicine spoon past her lips, though her teeth stayed clenched. He spanked her until green snot oozed down her red face. Still she refused to take the pink liquid. I felt sure he would kill her, the way he yelled. His eyes glowed; he sucked his teeth. Small, she remained stubborn, and panic rose in me—anger too. A child, who needed to be coaxed and loved the way children do. Only a monster would not see that. He had no patience, not even for Baby Carmen, who was his and small.

I acted on instinct. Save the drowning girl.

"Leave her alone!" I yelled, pushing myself between father and daughter.

How it worked, I do not know. I like to imagine it was the fire in my eyes that made him back away, throw the amoxicillin bottle against the wall, storm out. Whatever it was, he left the house. I listened, relieved when I heard his car peel out. Mom sat, her head in her hands, trembling at the table.

I picked up the bottle and put my hand on Carmen's tiny shoulder.

"Are you ready to take your get better juice now?" Softly-spoke.

She shook her head no, without even looking up.

"Hey Mom," I said. "Do you remember that time I had to get a shot for a really bad asthma attack? And I literally climbed the walls trying to get away from the needle?"

"Yeah, I do." She looked up, sniffed. "We tried holding you. They had to bring in two nurses. They had to strap you down."

"I know! I was so scared. I hate shots. Can't even stand to watch them on TV. But did I ever tell you how glad I was after? Thankful to be breathing free again?" I pulled a chair next to Mom, sat down and wrapped my arms around her in a hug.

"You know I love you, right Mom?"

Carmen climbed out of her chair and came to where she stood beside us, her fat little fingers on my thigh.

"I love you too, Carmen." I hugged her tight, held her long. "You ready to try taking your medicine?"

She nodded yes, her eyes sad and round, and I picked up the spoon and held it out for her to grab. She wiped her tears, sniffling, picked up the spoon and took her medicine. She made a sour face that bloomed into a smile once she swallowed.

The three of us stayed in the kitchen for a while, Mom and I too stunned to move on. Carmen seemed to have forgotten the incident, talking in her partly comprehensible toddler way, pretending to feed medicine to Mom and me in turns with the empty syringe.

"Mmm…" we said sometimes, or shaking our heads no, and "Will it taste bad?" to which she always replied no, it tasted like bubble gum or ice cream or chicken. No matter what she said it would taste like, it made all three of us laugh.

Mom went to get a couple of hair ties and a brush, then sat next to me, gesturing for me to turn my face away from her. The moment she started brushing my hair, she began to speak in more than jags. She told stories about when she was a little girl, how she envied her sister. I have seen pictures of Mom as a girl: pale skin, dark hair, summer sky-blue eyes. Looking at Carmen and Mom now, I saw how much they looked alike, felt hopeful for the fact that I could not see Ray in Carmen's eyes or cheeks or brow. All Mom.

I vowed in that love aftermath to be a kinder, better sister. Even that happened in increments, movements, not in one decisive blow.

Ray did not come home that night and I stayed up late, safely writing in my journal, not once distracted by the sound of his shoes on the floorboards outside my door, a creak that always stopped my breath, sank my beating heart. I wrote a story about two sisters who live in a spaceship and hate each other until they have to band together to defeat the rebels. They discover a plot against their mother, the queen. When they tell her about it, she does not believe them, chalking it up to their imagination. Scheming side by side on their own, they forget their petty annoyances and vow their allegiance to protect each other as long as they both shall live. The story was not any good. It sits among the stacks of notebooks full of forgotten words in my closet to this day, words that moved from my heart and mind to the tip of my pen to take form on the page.

Those early movements, so awkward and necessary.

SIX.

My body morphed into a new and bloated thing I was always conscious of. The Pits, as we called them, became a destination. Boys went there to ride motorbikes and watch girls. Girls went to watch boys, pose, and whisper-giggle. In June, the neighbor boy's cousin Daniel came to visit for the summer. He made me tongue-tied and dream-prone and so sure that if I could just find some way to let him know, he would be my happy-ending Romeo.

We played kick-the-can way past dark, until we had to rummage through kitchen drawers for flashlights and sneak out of windows after pretending to fall asleep. One night, huddled behind a rhododendron bush, watching Joe (who was IT) base-hog, Daniel took my sweaty hand in his and kissed me, then ran for it and touched base while Joe was tagging another kid. I did not get close to him again that night, but he did wave to me before we all headed back into our houses.

I waited for his appearance the next morning, sitting on the porch sheltered from the rain, watching the house I knew he had slept in, practicing what I might say when he emerged, skateboard under his arm, to greet me. From across the street, I saw his shaggy brown hair, his kind but a little bit troubled blue eyes. I imagined tongue-kissing and planning how, when summer ended, we would call or write, plan the next summer and the next.

But he did not come, and the rain did not stop. And after I had practiced my cartwheels and written four pages in my journal, I went in to lunch. I made grilled cheese and tomato soup with milk-not-water for Noah and me. Noah helped me with my math, then asked me if I wanted to make a character for his Dungeons and Dragons game. Feeling generous, I said *sure, why not* and he taught me about the number of sides on each dice (die he told me, if I only meant one). We rolled the stats for my Ranger and he told me I should join his game next weekend.

Noah only came around sometimes on weekends now. Mom explained how Grampa could take him to all his baseball practices, and how Noah wanted it this way. I knew it had more to do with the bloody nose Ray had given him over the D grade, and that Mom and Ray thought role-playing games summoned demons and so had burned all his D&D books and character sheets in the barrel out back.

I ran into Daniel at the pits holding another girl's hand. The girl down the street, Holly, who had woman breasts and, according to neighborhood legend, knew about sex. Holly was thirteen, with a perm and a pout. She carried a mint-green boom box on a strap over her shoulder and swore.

I asked Mom if I could stay at Granny and Grampa's house so I could test out the character Noah helped me roll, only I told her we were going to play cards and eat pizza. She said yes and did not ask Ray like she usually did. This felt like a little miracle, pleasantly surprised me, because Ray never let me sleep over anywhere.

Noah and his friends gathered in the basement. Granny had let them drag in a discarded couch and two recliners. His friend Sam brought his own bean bag chair and they all brought sleeping bags. Not that they would sleep much. These games notoriously went all night and left Noah dark-eyed and crabby the next day.

Six older boys and me, all of them talking at once.

The campaign involved all of us trekking through a haunted wood to recover a sacred scroll. Noah, our dungeon master, explained how the magic of the scroll might save us or unleash a host of monsters or both, but we had no choice. The wizard consulted in the last game thrust this mission upon us. It was the only path we had traveled that did not lead to a dead end.

John, a skinny, pimple-faced boy wearing an Iron Maiden tee shirt and drinking a two-liter of knock-off cola, protested.

"What's the fun of a campaign without choices?"

The others grumbled their agreement. A couple of them threatened to leave the game.

Noah called them pussies, and reminded them that he knew what he was doing, and they acquiesced long enough to roll the dice.

We battled a horde of orcs and snuck past a dragon on our way to an inn where we hoped to meet a thief who would tell us the quickest route to the shrine where a clan of warriors guarded the scroll. As the dice rolled, arguments ignited and fizzled. I lay on my belly on a sleeping bag next to John and Ben.

The boys swore and smoked cigarettes by the rhododendrons out back. Some sipped cheap beer from paper bags. One boy or another got up to piss from time to time, making a show of it. *Gotta take a leak, gotta drain the lizard, gotta pay the water bill.* One pissed in an empty bottle because he did not want to go out in the rain.

In game, the floorboards of the inn creaked. We all ordered pints and surveyed the room full of rotten teeth and shifty eyes.

"Arielle gets up on the table to make a speech," Noah said, not even looking at me.

John and Ben dragged a milk crate over for me to stand on.

"What's the speech supposed to be about?" I asked. "I don't know what to say."

"It doesn't matter," Noah said. "You are just creating a diversion while Rohan confronts the man in the green hooded cape playing solitaire in the corner."

I stood on the milk crate and said *Ladies and Gentlemen*, then paused to think what to say next, feeling the boys' eyes on me and wishing I was invisible.

I started again, made up a story about how we had traveled to this inn, lost many comrades along the way, how I wanted to make a toast to those who had lost hope and I hoped that everyone would join me.

"The crowd stands in anticipation, their glasses raised," Noah said. "You've got their attention."

I remembered the trick Noah taught me about how to pick a spot on the wall to stare at to create an illusion of eye contact for teachers who assign book reports and care a lot about that. I turned one horde of orcs into three and exaggerated the size and length of the dragon before

I took another breath. I threw in an evil witch and a child pretending to be lost who was really a spy looking to poison us. I paused, hoping that would do.

It did. The boys clapped. I think they may have been surprised. After I spoke, Rohan (John) rolled and Noah successfully confronted the man in the corner, the thief we sought.

The room smelled of dirty socks and cigarettes. Dying fluorescent lights dully flickered. I was cold and I unzipped my sleeping bag and wrapped it around me.

We left the inn and returned to the path, but then Noah hit our warrior with a seizure out of nowhere, which led to tense rolling of dice and ended in a real life wrestling match because the warrior wanted to roll a new character.

Once the rolling of new characters opened up, it was a free-for-all, and the rest of the night became about creating a new persona better than the last one.

"Do you wanna roll a character?" John asked.

He lay on his stomach and pulled out a shoebox full of colored pencils for drawing his elf magic-user.

I did not really have a handle on my one character, but I said *sure, why not.*

Handful after handful of chips, cup after cup of soda, understanding some percentage of the long-winded explanations of why high dexterity would bode well for me but not as much as high intelligence, I did not think much of John's hand on my knee while he coached me. After the lights went out, three hours before sunrise, I closed my eyes and almost fell asleep. I felt the sleeping bag zipper give and a hand creep in, and my breath caught. *Not here, not here too.* My body stiffened in that way I tried to communicate disinterest without words. He kept prodding, feeling my small breasts and rubbing my inner thigh, not speaking. The silence in the dark basement closing in.

What if I screamed *stop* or *don't* or *who the hell do you think I am?*

I closed my eyes and tried to think of being somewhere else, any place else, unable to settle on somewhere that would save me. He moaned and I rolled over, feigning sleep. I prayed for morning to come. When it did, I had not slept, and my stomach ached. I crept up the stairs, hoping not to wake a single sleeping boy.

Spinning, spinning, spinning.

Granny stood in the kitchen, turning slices of ham in the pan.

"You hungry?"

"Uh-uh," I said, settling into the chair next to where her cigarette burned in the ashtray.

I never attended another game night, even though Noah asked me. *Why?* He wanted to know. I had seemed to enjoy it.

That same school year, a boy in my class named Artie tried to convince me to lift my shirt for him and his older brother behind the dumpsters at the back of the school.

"Just climb in," he said, pointing to an empty burning barrel. "Then pop up and lift up your shirt."

"It's no big deal," he added.

I did not want to, but he was right about it being no big deal, and he would not leave me alone so I said, yes, I would do it.

The memory of this moment sticks with me still, one of the many which my monkey mind conjures up sometimes when I am feeling low down, and figure I have always been weak-willed and willing. Like the time Artie pinched my ass and left a blueberry-sized bruise. Like Ray's visits in the night. Like John at game night. Like every time a boy teased me or pulled my braid.

The year I turned twelve, Mom threw a pizza party at Shakey's Pizza Shack. Three of the five friends I invited showed. Noah brought his handsome friend Robert who we stole glances at and whispered about, who I didn't know then, not like I did after my first and last game night.

Our hair tied up in scrunchies, my three friends and I stood around the soda fountain making our own versions of a graveyard: coke, sprite, orange or root beer, coke, sprite, some variation of a little of everything. We wore over-sized sweatshirts with tight jeans, earrings that dangled almost to the shoulders.

Dad lingered like a ghost at the edge of the party. He had been back in town for a month or so, and we could not even make small talk. He had traveled some, and spent a couple of years in prison for something no one would talk about. His cheeks were hollow and his eyes looked like reflections in spoons. He stayed through the whole party, staying close to Granny and Grampa, though even that must have been awkward for him. Mom made a yellow cake with chocolate frosting and we sang Happy Birthday before it was time to open gifts. I opened Dad's first, a crystal necklace in the shape of a heart that came with a business card inside. *It's programmed for you*, he said, which I did not understand and felt skeptical about. But I would wear the damn thing and tell everyone it was programmed for me as if I believed it and knew what that meant.

We played Galaga, air hockey, and skee ball, took our piles of tickets to trade in for a prize. I had five hundred three tickets, enough for two pixy sticks and a chinese finger trap.

Still angry at Dad for putting me on a bus, but intrigued by the mystery he exuded, the way he challenged so many of the rules I had been given for living just by being there, being him. I watched him, wanting to say something, anything that might start a pool of knowing. But all I could manage was "How are you?" and "Thank you. I love it." And then his physical self, tall, thin-limbed, tan, shades of me for sure, always with a cup of his own in his hand that somehow I knew was the source of the pine scent on his breath when he hugged me, kissed my cheek.

"I've got to go," he said, squeezing my hand, words stuck in his throat, or so I imagined that he, like me, wished he could say more.

At school—everywhere—we girls moved in a party, curious, flirting with each other, throwing glimpses behind us to check for witnesses to our emergence. The boys would soon be picking us off one by one, but these were the times for braiding each other's hair and practice kissing each other at slumber parties.

Crush faded into crush in a cycle that would spin out into

adulthood, the heartbreak mattering more with each experience, not less like one would think, an irony many a pop idol has cashed in on.

I had a crush on my sixth grade teacher who perched on a wooden stool to read us all of *Roll of Thunder, Hear My Cry* while I watched the orange leaves blow off the trees and the November rain flood the playground.

Boys trying to get to base. Girls trying to fall in love. These initial forays into romance are never anything but doomed, though sometimes sweet to remember. Like Jerry, who rode The Zipper with me at the Puyallup Fair. We split an entire bag of blue cotton candy and held hands in the back seat of his parents' minivan on the way back home. When Jerry started picking flowers for Mindy and writing her love notes I mourned only for one day before I started coaching Mindy to go for it.

We girls would ride across town and push our bikes up the tallest hill in Aberdeen just for that thirty-second weightlessness of legs-splayed gliding down. The seed of movement planted, the impulse grew and grew. We would leave on rides in the morning and not return until dinner time. We rode to each other's houses, across busy streets and through alleyways. I would ride out alone too, and learned it took an hour and a half to ride the eight miles across town if I did not stop to skip rocks or hang from the monkey bars at Midway Park.

I rode a blue ten-speed with a water bottle holder I put on myself. I learned to put my chain back on when it slipped, and how to ride with no hands. I learned how to switch between gears and how to signal truck drivers to prompt them to honk their horns.

One Saturday, Mindy and I rode to the woods and back. We went to Benjamin Park on the edge of town to pick huckleberries on the nature trail, and cross the swinging bridge. We packed lunch and scrounged $4.23 from change in our junk drawers and couch cushions.

When two girls get together for an adventure like ours, something softens between them, secrets spill out. Mindy opened first. She had a crush. Her mom and dad had been fighting. A lot. She worried they might divorce. Her mom bought her a training bra and made her wear it. I told her I missed my brother, but not why he left. I told her my parents also fought, but not about Ray's temper. I told her I had a crush too. She asked who. I said you tell me first. We agreed to count to three and then blurt it out together.

Gasp! Same boy.

Mindy had dimples deep and darling. For school lunch, her mom cut the crusts off her sandwiches and packed her a Zinger or a Ho-Ho, plus a drink and chips. She seemed to have everything, which is why I never understood why she lied so much and cheated at games. When

I could get her alone she did not act like the impress-everybody-else
Mindy, just the curious Mindy and the you're-the-best-friend-ever Mindy.

We wheeled across town and back, and on the way home coasted
four times down the tallest hill. We rode standing up and *hey look, no
legs*, feet off the pedals, legs splayed. We pedaled backward and sang the
words to Bryan Adams' *Reckless*.

The firing of muscles, the turning of wheels, the way I covered
ground. That movement, and the movement of a pen across a page,
writing free and without stopping, filled a new and urgent desire.

I had a few close girlfriends who were always fighting amongst
themselves, singling out one girl or another, though most of us had
known each other since before we learned to read. I took a turn being
singled out the summer before starting seventh grade. I was not even
sure what I had done.

"If you don't know, I'm not telling you," Mindy said and hung up
the phone.

I did not know, but I knew how this game worked. Every month
or so, someone new was targeted to be ostracized, usually because one or
another girl was jealous of her. Maybe I did not care, I thought. Maybe
I would be happier without their drama. I could do whatever I wanted

and would not have to worry what anyone thought. I wrote all this in my journal, including a poem about how we look at things all the time without really seeing them. Then, I went for a bike ride.

The sun was high and it was a humid 94 degrees. That was hot for any day in Aberdeen, let alone a mid-July day. I craved a 7-Eleven Slurpee and then, who knew? I had a whole day ahead of me.

Rolling down First Street, I pedaled through a crowd of kids who had run into the street to escape the hose some dad-man had turned on them.

"No! No!" They yelled, laughing. Not meaning it.

I passed the house where the cat lady lived, the house with the bright purple door, several yards strewn with plastic play equipment in disrepair, passed the Rainbow Garden Day Care Center (run out of a house), and the elementary school I had graduated from in June. I traveled across ten neighborhood blocks to get to where 7-Eleven decorated the main drag with neon splendor. I parked my bike and bumped through the swinging door.

I saw them congregated at the Slurpee machines: Mindy, Laura, Kim, Carrie, and Jennifer.

A sharp intake of breath. "Hey, guys."

They said nothing, pretended they did not see me. I pulled a sixteen-ounce cup and poured a Pina Colada (favorite), noting, without making eye contact, the look of disgust Mindy aimed at me. I paid and left, keeping my cool. Out of sight, around the corner from the store, I took a sip of the Slurpee. I tasted nothing, tossed the cup in the trashcan and rode my bike home. I cried all the way, cried in waves that crashed and receded, then crashed again. And yet there was a certain sense in this, in taking my turn as outcast, the payoff being the days—most days—when I was on the inside, when together we lost our identities to the group of girls who, though individually terrified, created myths of power together. This cruelty made sense, unlike other cruelties I sullenly tried to understand and could not, such as the images of starving children shown alongside 1-800 numbers on television.

Because it was summer, I was outcast longer. Out of sight, out of mind. They did not see me and so did not have to face the truth: the error had always been slight, unintentional, human. I spent five solitary weeks drinking Slurpees, bike riding, writing poems and observations in my journal, and doing cartwheels on the lawn in hopes that the neighbor boy's sweet-eyed cousin would wander by.

I loved the way my breath caught with every cartwheel. I believed I was a princess waiting for a prince whose kiss would feel like one of those cartwheels.

Waiting is easy when you are secluded in your tower for the summer, writing in your journal, watching reruns, and pedaling free through the neighborhood. One day I met a girl a couple years younger catching tadpoles by the ditch. She had made a daisy crown for her head, so I supposed she was a princess too. I helped her fill three jars with tadpoles and then carry them back to her house, where her mom made us grilled cheese sandwiches and we watched Road Runner.

Emma lived in one side of a sad gray duplex with her mom and three cats named Bo, Jo-Jo and Skinny. She thought I was smart, and her laugh sounded smooth as marbles. I spent the last summer of my childhood following Emma's imagination through the neighborhood, taking funny pictures of her cats with a Polaroid camera and listening to her mom's warning about boys and kidnappers.

Emma's mom was sick, though Emma did not say what ailed her. I thought maybe cancer, because she chain-smoked. She sat in her blue robe in the corner by the window reading magazines or just staring out the window. She whisper-hummed a tune I recognized but could not place. I wish I could tell you what happened to her, whether she got better or what happened to Emma, who she grew up to be. But after that summer, I lost track of Emma. Once I started middle school, I could not go back to the leisurely world where anything you imagined could be true.

The Lighthouse Drive-In Restaurant sign beamed from the corner where I would catch the bus to my first day of Miller Junior High, like an arm waved to oncoming traffic, with a lit arrow and a few missing bulbs. Owned by a churchy family, The Lighthouse stood for the light that shines in all of us. *This little light of mine, I'm gonna let it shine.* The Lighthouse served the best thick, crinkle-cut fries that came with a small plastic container of special sauce, all for $1.07 after tax.

Right across from The Lighthouse, a Christian Scientist church loomed tall and brown, and mysterious because I never saw anyone go inside. Panning out from there: a discount grocery store, A Jehovah's Witness church, and three taverns.

The first morning of middle school, I walked to the bus stop alone. Mindy stood by herself in new clothes, her hair in a ponytail to one side. Her cheeks blushed with the cold morning air, betraying not a hint of her 7-Eleven confidence.

"Hey," I said.

"Are you excited?" She asked.

"A little. A little scared, too."

A small vulnerability shared between us erased an entire summer of exile. We giggled together on the bus, helped each other find our lockers and our classes, passed notes, and ended the day at the bus stop, sharing Lighthouse Fries and stories.

I wish I could say I learned some lesson from my estrangement, that it taught me compassion for the outcast, but it did not. I wanted to fit in like everyone else. Being accepted again only made me work harder to stay in the good graces of my friends.

"Mr. Tall is a jerk," Mindy complained.

"Yeah," I said, though I liked Mr. Tall and his low tolerance for screw-offs.

"I'm not talking to Laura," she said, picking at her pizza slice, chewing on a fingerful of cheese.

"What happened?"

Eyes rimmed with blue eye shadow, her pink lips shimmered. "She lies. I'm tired of it."

Of course, I found this ridiculous, but said nothing. Laura did lie. All the time. She had been lying since we met her at seven, and we had taken a blood oath with her at ten. It was like accusing her for being the oldest (she was), or the clumsiest (she was), or the most boy-crazy (she was). Plus everyone of us lied in our own artful way.

For the next week when Laura tried to talk to us we walked on, pretending we could not hear. I did not answer her calls except once, when I told her *listen, you should really talk to Mindy and work things out.* I am not proud of this, and sometimes I wonder if we were not all trying to blow up our friendship. We would not get Laura back. Before Mindy decided to forgive her, she had found a new group of friends who appreciated her more. We were all finding groups who appreciated us more. The circumstances of age, gender, and being zoned for the same elementary school had thrown us together. Just as we were coming to an age of thinking for ourselves, we moved to a school with entirely new possibilities friendship-wise. A clean slate.

I met Jill and Susanna in Mr. Tall's English class. I missed a day of school, and when I returned I had been put in a group with them for the infamous poetry anthology project, a six week project followed by another two weeks of presentations about the six-week process. In the end, this particular project would make up most of my grade for the quarter. I got lucky. Around the room students moaned and balked. They took apart their pens and signaled to their friends across the room, a sort of S.O.S. saying, *Poetry! Why?*

But at our table, the more we flipped through the project packet discussing the types of poems we had to choose from, the more the excitement built, an island abuzz with possibility amid chaos and despair.

Mindy started turning out for sports and spending time with the girls who carried gym bags from class to class. We had planned to live on the same block some day, take our children to the same parks, and have the same really great jobs at the same place in advertising, record production, or law. We had promised we would live our lives hip to hip, like our Barbies had. We had snuck over to Laura's house one day in fifth grade at lunch to press our pin-pricked fingers together and sip from Laura's mother's wine. We were blood sisters, but our breaking apart was as easy and inevitable as our coming together had been.

Jill and Susanna filled the space left. Overfilled it really, because of middle school. We felt independent compared to the girls who fixed each other's hair and lipstick in the bathroom that they could not walk into without each other. We did not wear the right shade of eyeshadow, the right brand of jeans, or we did not wear eye shadow at all. In retrospect, I see how we still wore the same off-brand of jeans as each other, the same off-shade of eyeshadow and sought each other's company and approval in all things.

Jill lived up on the hill with her grandparents. Her mom lived in Alaska. Jill did not like to talk about her except to say that she never heard from her, a statement punctuated by her downcast eyes. Over time I would pull out a few more details. Mom liked beer and heroin, had never taken to motherhood, though for a while she did try. Jill had her

mom's thick, fine stringy blond hair, her long legs, and her foul-mouthed

penchant for brutal truth, as Jill called it.

Susanna lived in the housing projects with her doting mom

who worked a CNA job just to make it month to month, but who still

made time to sew clothes and drive her places. Her mom claimed not to

know for sure the identity of Susanna's dad, but Susanna did not believe

her. Susanna had made it her personal mission to crack the case. In the

meantime, she kept a journal addressed to him next to her mattress on

the floor.

We had no money, no cars, nowhere to be when we were not at

school. So we spent our time sitting in each other's bedrooms, writing

stories and dreaming of where and who we would be some day. We

watched movies that were frightening, like Cujo, or tragic, like Terms of

Endearment, and gave each other manicures.

The secrets became more and more shared. We offered

confidences as tokens of friendship and insurance that we would be

friends forever. Jill told us when Mark Wilson felt her up, when she

planned to go all the way with him, and when she had gone all the way

with him.

"I don't see what the big deal is," she said, giggling. "Don't get your hopes up. It's not what you'd think with all the fuss around it."

Then, one winter-break day in eighth grade, I actually convinced Mom and Ray to let me stay all night at Jill's, even though they never said yes to my staying over places. They only let me have friends over at our house. I felt liked I had escaped, and maybe I would never have to go back because I could see the snow piling up outside the window. Jill, Susanna and I were sitting around in our sweats, writing to prompts like "write about a time you felt lonely" and "black cat".

I did not tell them directly, but I wrote about the lonely period of the evening, waiting to see if Ray would push my door open, tread silent into my room. I said "he" not Ray, but they knew.

"Is that true?" Jill asked.

"You have to tell someone," Susanna added.

I shrugged and no one said a word for a long, painful period of silence.

"Well, I was going to save this for later," Jill said. "But I think we could all use a shift in perspective right now." Jill took a joint and a lighter out of her pocket.

"Since when do you smoke?" Susanna asked.

Mark gave her the joint, she explained. She had only smoked

once, she said, with him. He said he liked sex better high and she did too, she told us. We found ourselves in a perfect moment for risking our identities further. We had so many secrets and sins already. Why not one more?

We smoked the whole joint, giggling, got dressed and walked through two inches of snow to an open field where we rolled and packed snowballs to hurl at each other. We did not talk more about the secret I had let slip, but the truth of it vibrated between us, and each snowball thrown hurled toward an invisible target. The truth deepened a well building in each of us, a well of experiences in which our bodies were strange and dangerous.

SEVEN.

By the time I started high school, I found a way to tell Mom about Ray. I left a note for her, signed it *Love, Your Daughter, Eve*. But she did not leave him or kill him as I had half-hoped. She did not send me to live with Noah at Granny and Grampa's as I prayed she would, as I thought at first she was because that is where she drove me to sleep for the night that turned into three. For a long time after, the adults in my life grew shame-faced and whispering like I could not handle what they were talking about, like I was not entitled to know and have a say.

Mom believed me, but she also believed it was just me, and that Carmen surely was safe. Ray cried and apologized and promised her this was so.

"Well, you can't just go on like nothing happened," I overheard Granny tell Mom. "You can't keep her there with him."

Who came up with the idea of contacting Dad I do not know. Mom showed up at Granny's, her face pale. She sat down on the couch beside me, looking like she had swallowed a lie.

"We've been thinking," she started. "We've been thinking that maybe you need a little time away and that it might be nice for you to get to know your Dad."

Some time away? Get to know my Dad? What I did not hear her say is *Ray is leaving, you can come home*, so I could not say anything, only look at her like the stranger she was already becoming. Was I being punished?

"I think this will be best for everyone." She squeezed my lifeless hand and brushed my hair away from my face.

"Don't you think if Dad wanted me to live with him he would have at least visited? Returned my letters? I don't even know him."

"Which is why this will be good for both of you."

My heart raced. I felt dizzy, like I might get sick or float up to the ceiling. How had this become about Dad?

No, she said, she was not choosing Ray. We were a family. I had been hurt and needed some time away. Ray needed to pray and see a counselor. We would all be back together soon. Back together soon was not what I wanted, at all. But she could not hear me through her tears and her fear of being alone or falling apart or whatever it was. What could I do but agree, as though I actually had a choice?

When I hauled my bags into Dad's silver Mercedes to move to the apartment he had rented in Aberdeen, I looked for the inconvenience I must have been to him in every glance, every gesture, every effort to make small talk.

"Nice car," I said.

"It's my boyfriend's," he said.

"Jim?" I asked, thinking *the fucker who talked you into putting me on a bus.*

"No," he said. "We broke up ages ago. His name is Rich, you'll meet him soon."

So much I wanted to say, wanted to ask. Why had he put me on that bus? Was it something I had done? Why hadn't he come to see me? Did he know I wanted to be a writer? That I had won the spelling bee in second grade? That I hated liver and onions, but loved asparagus and chicken adobo?

"Hmmm. I wouldn't have known."

He ignored my hurt-jab. "I live right next to your school, so this is going to work out well. You can walk to school. Until you get a license. Do you know how to drive?"

"No." You should know I don't, I thought.

"Well, sounds like I need to teach you, then. You want to be independent, right?"

"I am independent." I crossed my arms and sunk deeper into the leather seat, crushed a tissue box on the floorboard with my shoe.

"Then, you'd better learn to drive."

"Does Rich live with you?" I asked.

"Oh, no," he said and I wondered at the *Oh*.

When we arrived at his apartment, he made grilled cheese sandwiches and tomato soup. We ate in relative silence. I commented on his black stoneware bowls with little kanji symbols on the sides that I assumed read Peace, Love, Happiness or something like that. They felt sturdy and strange in my hands.

"These are nice bowls," I said. "They match and everything."

"What's your favorite subject in school?" He asked, unruffled at my disdain.

As father and daughter, we should have been able to do better. I know the questions I should have asked. But I held back for fear I would not like the answers or, worse, he would not answer me at all. I assume that he must have held back too, that he wanted to know the things about me he had missed, that I had kept locked away. And yet he knew something terribly personal, and I had not been the one who told him. And that made me angry at him.

Dressed in denim jacket and jeans, popped collar on a mint green polo shirt, I ate two bowls of soup and two sandwiches, then asked to be shown to my room.

The room was as spare as the rest of the house, a pine futon bed and a four-drawer walnut dresser with a simple beige-shaded lamp atop. Plenty of white walls to stare at as I lay in the dark, wishing the awkwardness away (or if that could not be, that I could jump this life for another try).

The next morning dad made eggs, bacon, and hash-browned potatoes, and he cranked all the blinds open so that shafts of light were shining in from all angles of the house to illuminate breakfast. Our small talk came easier now as we created a language that would allow us to be in the present together, shielded from the past. He gave me the funny pages from his newspaper and pretended to need help with his crossword puzzle.

A week or so into our reunion, just when we had settled into a routine that was more like two roommates who like each other than parent and child, Dad started spending nights away. Jill or sometimes Susanna would come stay with me. More often Jill, because her parents were more lenient about letting her out on school nights.

Jill cussed and smoked and read sexy books she passed on to me when she finished them. We fed each other writing prompts and then read our work aloud to each other. We watched MTV and listened to entire U2 albums in stunned silence. When she brought big bottles of beer and joints in little plastic baggies, I said yes because I never wanted to say no to her.

One night we stayed up late watching a B-movie called *Night of the Comet* propped up on pillows, eating popcorn and drinking beer on my bed. We were giddy, open to anything.

"Have you ever kissed a girl?" Jill asked, the dark mole on her right cheek a suggestion.

I said no but I had thought about it, wondered what it was like, explained that I was not into girls or anything. I just wondered.

What followed was fumbled, inexperienced, incomplete, and confusing, but awakening at the same time. The smell of her Suave-washed hair, the tentative way we touched, pausing to gauge the other's reaction. Running my tongue across her ear lobe, holding her breast, kissing her neck until she moaned.

We fell asleep naked, spooning, talking about boys.

"He's a nice guy," I said, talking about Zach, my crush.

"Are you sure?" she asked.

Emboldened by the run of the house I had, a week later we invited him and his friend to smoke joints and listen to The Velvet Underground. Zach and James, giddy to find us alone, feeling powerful and free.

"So your dad is never home?"

"He makes appearances," I said, nonchalant.

"Wow. That's really cool." His friend's two cents.

I first noticed Zach in Spanish class, when he smiled and said *you have really nice eyes, can I borrow a pencil?* Tonight, though, I could see he had set that smile on Jill. He could hardly take his eyes off her. His hands followed.

I drank too much and the room started to spin. When Jill asked *do you mind* I said no, only half aware of what it was she thought I might protest, but knowing when Zach pulled her into the other room by one arm, looking for the prize at the other end.

Left alone with me, James bragged about how he broke his arm in a mosh pit last week, asked if I wanted to sign his cast. I signed *Love, Eve* and drew a tree and a heart with an arrow through it, one of four or five things I could draw.

We talked awkwardly over sex sounds from Dad's room. James had gumball-shaped blue eyes and spoke to fend off silence, adding chatter to the noise from the other room, which is why I kissed him. After that, I kept saying yes because I could not think of a reason not to.

We ought to do a better job of teaching girls to say no instead of teaching them a million ways to acquiesce, because to acquiesce is a kind of movement too. And if a girl is not careful, she finds herself less and less inclined to move of her own accord.

All of this alone time was weird at first, and it inspired nervous energy. I paced, wrote long reflective journal entries containing conversations with myself, mostly critical, with Gatsby-esque lists for self-advancement.

1. Write every day.

2. Eat healthier.

3. Speak up!

I cooked the three things I knew how to cook: stir fry, top ramen, and grilled cheese sandwiches. I listened to Joni Mitchell and Bob Dylan cassettes over and over, and read most of what I checked out from the library, including *Fear of Flying* and *Even Cowgirls Get the Blues*.

Out walking one evening through a neighborhood park just as the sun dipped down for the day, panic inhabited me. At the time, I thought it spelled death or insanity for sure, and all the worst possible scenarios, my heart racing--*what is wrong with me?* I ran-walked home, locked the door behind me, and commenced pacing. None of this helped, and I could not stop my thoughts from circling the drain of fear and insecurity, no matter what I tried to think of or not think of, whether I sat still or moved. I tried making tea, taking a bath, and in time the adrenaline wore off. I slipped into nervous dreaming.

The next day I worried it would happen again, only this time in front of people. I spent third period locked in a bathroom stall staring at the words Eat Cock written in silver paint marker. I left school early, went home and bolted the door behind me.

I spread a blanket out on the floor and took out a yoga book Dad had given me, that I had set aside, having poked fun at the pure white head-to-toe leotard getup worn by the cover model. The directions oozed sexism. Give an extra stretch when you are reaching to the highest shelf in your kitchen while making dinner, when you are sweeping or mopping your floor, the book advised.

Now, I turned to it. Wasn't it rumored that yoga can relax you?
Since I was sure I was losing my mind, I had to try something.

I sat on the floor and opened the book. In Simhasana, you sit on
your heels, hands on your knees, then you fold forward, eyes surprise-
wide, tongue all out, exhaling loudly before returning back to upright. I
did it, and it felt really silly at first. By the third round I felt a possibility
of confidence. For the next pose I lay prone on the floor, then with an
inhale lifted my torso up, hands under shoulders, elbows tucked to ribs,
solar plexus lifted to the ceiling, exhaled to release. I lay on my belly, head
turned to one side, feeling the pulse of energy move up my spine. I did—
well, tried to do—every pose in the book, including the meditation at the
end. My mind never stilled, but I managed to keep two butt bones rooted
to the ground, and observed my own shallow breath getting slower and
deeper.

I had not found a cure for this new unrest, but I had found a
possibility if I practiced. And I did practice, yoga book propped next to
where I practiced. Right there on the carpet, because I did not have a mat
or know where to find one. I read descriptions of each pose and tried
again and again, checking the black and white photographs, reading the
descriptions.

When Jill first asked me to go running with her, I laughed—*no way*. But then I re-opened the subject a few days later.

"When did you start running?" I asked her.

"I used to run with my dad," she said. "Before he died."

Jill's dad died of cancer when she was nine, so she had no tolerance for me complaining about my dad.

I hesitated. "All right, I'll try it."

"Great!" she said, enthusiastically.

The next morning she knocked on my door. There she stood, flushed and ready.

"Come on, let's do this. Don't even try to get out of it."

I ran maybe a mile on that first run, and I did get a little wheezy by the end. But I also felt hope and calm, sweet calm. The rhythm of my feet on the earth, the smell of dirt and trees, the feeling I could outrun or run down anything. I could.

This is not the happy ending. I had a long way still to go before I could say that I saved myself from drowning after all. I would run sometimes and practice yoga sometimes and begin to understand this body I had been born to.

EIGHT.

Heartbreak, breaking hearts, attachment, being the object of attachment, in no particular pattern. First, Zach with the blue eyes who Jill now called boyfriend and had gone all moon-eyed over.

"James really likes you," Jill offered.

"I don't know," I said, French-braiding her hair for the party.

Zach picked us up in his red Ford truck as planned. Jill sat in the middle, her hand moving from his knee to his crotch the whole way, giggling at his story about how he convinced his English teacher she lost his paper, even though he had not turned it in. She giggled when he revved his engine and rolled down his window to shout *pussy* to a car full of wide-eyed, flushed-faced friends who were also listening to Nine Inch Nails. I did not know this Jill, and I did not like her. I quietly blamed Zach.

"James really likes you," Zach said.

"So I hear." I turned the volume knob four clicks higher.

At the party we made drinks in the kitchen, then parted ways. They went into the living room. I went out the slider onto the back porch of somebody's house by the river, surrounded by evergreens, watched over by the moon and the stars.

The smokers congregated, drunk-talking. Two big-haired, made-up girls in jean jackets and miniskirts eyed me curiously when I stepped out in my flannel and long johns under cut-offs. I wore no make-up, and rarely bothered to put contacts in. I wore black-framed glasses and the nose ring I had gotten at the mall the day Jill and I ducked out of class early to find a copy of *Leaves of Grass* at the bookstore.

I bummed a smoke from the tall boy in the corner wearing harness boots and a sneer.

"Thanks," I said, taking my first drag, hoping I did not choke.

"Do you smoke?" He said.

I looked at the cigarette dangling from my hand and then back at him, sarcastically.

"No," he said. "Do you smoke?" He pulled a baggie out of his pocket just enough to show a wad of green, then tucked it back.

"All the time," I lied.

We stepped off the porch and walked toward the moon, out into the woods behind the house. Twigs snapped underfoot while a neighbor's dog barked a warning. We found a small clearing with three cedar stump stools to choose from. When he held the lighter to the bowl so I could take a hit, his face lit up with shadows. The long scar above his eyes glowed. I could not hold back the fit of coughing that followed that lung burn.

"Good shit, right?" He said, taking a hit himself, holding the smoke in for eleven seconds, by my count.

I finished the tumbler of fuzzy navel I had made nice and strong. I said yes and when he offered me another hit. I took the pipe.

"Put your thumb over the carb," he said, holding the lighter flame ready.

I wanted to pass eleven, but I exhaled at nine. He took my hand in his, tracing shapes along my palm with his index finger. He complained about school. Auto shop was his only useful class. I nodded not because I related, but because I understood how others felt that way. When I read novels and wrote papers on them, teachers wrote comments like *strong voice* and *nice detail*. I was good at school.

"I can't wait to be done with all of it," he said. He was a senior, and graduation awaited like a god-given right.

"What will you do after you graduate?" I asked.

"I don't know yet. Get the hell out of here, that's for sure."

He traced letters on my palm and I imagined he had written *I love you*. I leaned in to kiss him, a warm open kiss which he returned, then pulled me closer to him. We stumbled back inside, laughing as we recounted an episode of Ren and Stimpy we had both seen, looking for another drink. One moment laughing, turning down the volume of everyone around me except Jeff, the next struck by a gaze from across the room, a gaze that assumed too much. James.

The way James looked at me as if I owed him something may have inspired what I did next. Also the pot, the booze, the moon, and the barking dog.

"Let's get out of here," I tugged the sleeve of Jeff's leather jacket.

I left without telling Jill where I was going, wound up wrapped up in sleeping bags on the floor of Jeff's parents' attic full of old furniture and piles of photo albums not even packed away in boxes, a street light shining through one octagon-shaped window. What happened there still surprises me to think about. I ran fingernails up and down his back, leaving long streaks of red. He bit my earlobe just a little too hard. I bit his shoulder. Animal-love. I felt enough safety in him, just enough rage about James, Zach, and Jill.

Afterward, we talked, smoking cigarettes and leaning against each other's shoulders.

"So, you like it rough?" He asked.

"Not particularly. I guess you just bring that out of me."

We both laughed.

Surely I am falling in love, I thought.

Spinning, spinning, spinning.

But Jeff never did return my calls. And when I ran into him at a party a few months later, he did not even remember my name. Even though I had filled half a notebook with his name and written six sad love poems in order to heal the hurt I felt in the emptiness that followed his dropping me off the morning after, tracing his index finger across my open palm, and promising to call.

When I took a job working at Fast Burgers, I saw Dad even less than before. We left notes for each other, closing those notes with smiley faces and hearts. He put groceries in the fridge. I ate at work often, when I ate. Desire for food hit me in waves. A couple of days of crackers and apple slices, followed by a couple of days of burgers with the works and French fries. I liked both feelings of being starved and sickly full.

I graduated from high school a year and a half later by doing little more than showing up every day. I had only one plan for my future. I wanted to be a writer. I had written only one complete story, plus notebooks full of moments I had pulled from observation or imagination. I had no idea how to go about it, but I wanted to be a writer. I certainly did not need more school, I thought. All I needed was to read more and write every day. Why pay for an education when you have library books?

When Jill asked me to move with her to Olympia, I did not hesitate, and neither Mom nor Dad made waves. Jill's parents were paying her living costs and tuition at the community college, so she used the money she earned working at Skipper's as her recreation fund. She brought Zach with her, but did not tell her parents, as if he were just indefinitely sleeping over.

I found a job waitressing at a dive cafe downtown, a win for me because of the romance a writer working at a dive held in my mind. I would arrive hours before my shift and stay to drink coffee, smoke cigarettes, and scribble in journals. I would walk home alone in the dark because walking helped me think and brought me new ideas. I ran sporadically and did some yoga every day.

We drank and had people over. We smoked cigarettes and weed and sometimes hash. We tried Robitussin and pills left over from injuries, oral surgeries, or stuff taken from parents' medicine cabinets. A cook gave me a few hits of acid that *god knows why* I took on my way home from work one night as if I was not lonely enough already, as if I needed to spend the whole of an evening locked in my room imagining, then analyzing my trip in the sunrise of coming down. I took a walk, breathing in the cool morning air. It had been hot, even for August, too hot to sleep with more than a sheet. But on that morning, I felt the promise of fall in the air, a cool brush on my skin. I counted ten seagulls flying overhead. I crossed the bridge to downtown and saw two seals out in the water. I found a bench at Percival Landing and watched the sailboats docked and moving. I tried to cry, but nothing came.

Spinning, spinning, spinning.

After my shifts, I would find one group of customers or another to slide in with. Jeff, Dan, and Mike shared a house with three other college students. They sat always with their notebooks and pens out. They were putting together the first issue of a zine called Rorschach. They took turns coming up with prompts to write to and then share what they had written. They sat in the booth with the bench slanting on one side, where someone had carved the word RIOT into the table. I worked up the nerve to ask them about their writing so that I could say *hey I'm a writer too*, and then it was them I sat with.

I joined in on their writing sessions, listening to their pained poems and overwrought prose about fathers, femme fatales, and fate. I sensed a danger in the audience I provided for them, but I liked the only-woman attention. I liked having an audience for what I wrote.

One coffee-buzzed night I ordered home fries, sat down with these lit-boys, and took out my notebook.

"So what's the prompt tonight?"

Jeff grinned. "Write a sex scene that explores fetishism."

We wrote and shared the buzz of caffeine. Sex emboldened all of us. Ideas about sex we had only considered, we suddenly pretended to know about.

"The idea of monogamy is a tyranny, perpetuated by society to keep us shackled and ashamed," Mike said, pushing his glasses back up his nose, making chopping motions with his hands.

"Was that true for women too?" Especially for women, the boys all agreed. "What about pregnancy?" I asked. "A woman takes substantial risk in sex." Pregnancy can be avoided, came the response. Ideally, Mike said, children would not even belong to a single set of parents. All adults of a certain age would parent all the children in their community.

The idea of a mom and a dad like they are first gods, or our kings and queens? Absurd. We were all talking so much shit we did not know the first thing about.

Mike's eyes watched me every time he spoke the words *sex* or *fuck*. I unbraided my hair and shook it out, felt the weight of it down to my low back.

"It's hot in here," I said, taking off my flannel, exposing the red camisole I wore underneath, the tattoo of a yin-yang I had gotten last month right under where the knuckles of my hand sit when I recite the pledge of allegiance, hand over heart.

"We've got liquor. Wanna come over?" Jeff asked me.

Our waitress brought the check.

"Sure," I said, counting out change from my coin purse for the coffee.

We piled into Mike's beige beater sedan, me in the back between Jeff and Dan.

I would be lying if I said I did not know what we were headed toward. These were the days when being wanted was enough.

If I said no, I was a prude, I was scared, I was not as strong as I had put on after all. So I did not say no, not once that night.

I awoke on a creaky bed surrounded by the reek of alcohol sweat and the sound of snores, my head throbbing so bad I wished I could die. I gathered my clothes and slipped them on. I found my notebook and a pen. I sat in the corner writing until someone stirred.

"I really need to get home," I said to Mike when he sat up on the bed.

"What time is it?" he asked, barely able to open his eyes, wiping the corner of his mouth with the back of his hand.

They let dishes and mail pile up. They let ashtrays overflow. They left books, dirty laundry, and empty plates on the floor. The sooner I could leave this filthy place the better. He did drive me home, though he took a painfully long time getting around to it, and then he could not find his keys for twenty minutes.

He let me out at the curb, not even pulling into my apartment driveway completely.

"That was fun," he said, not looking at me. "Thanks."

I fake smiled, pecked his cheek. "Take care."

I took a long, hot shower and slept until early the following morning, when I woke in a panic.

Spinning, spinning, spinning.

I wanted to be part of this group, but I did not want to be part of this disembodiment. I wanted to hang out in cafes, smoke cigarettes, talk smart, and learn to write what would one day cause hearts to expand and sometimes break. Three days later I kissed Sam for the first time while sitting in the booth right across from Mike, Jeff, and Dan. I wanted them to know I had moved on, that it was not happening again. But, I was not sure I would be able to say no if they asked. I did also want to kiss Sam.

She had been flirting with me a while. Smart and funny, she also had a car and would wait around for hours to take me for a drive. She laughed so full and so often. She told people to fuck off if she felt like it. She wore long skirts and wrists full of bangles and read books by Betty Friedan and Anais Nin.

"You're such a lesbian and you don't even know it," She would say, laughing, nudging my shoulder with the flat palm of her hand.

The night I kissed her, she asked me to come home with her. Her room had its own entrance at the back of a house, like an apartment. She was nearly twenty, in her third year of college studying feminist literature and music. She wanted to make a living as a singer. When she played me her demo tapes I was sure she could do it. She had long, light brown hair and thin, soft pink lips that widened in a smile that spread to her bright green eyes and often finished with a cappuccino laugh, unusual and strong. She smelled sweet and earthy from the essential oils she dabbed on her wrists and rubbed in her hair and kept in a little vial hanging from the rear view mirror in her car.

That night we lay on her bed listening to all her favorite CDs, all powerful female voices like Tori Amos and Stevie Nicks, and I kissed her back, but stopped her always at the kiss and she let me. We fell asleep with our clothes on and in the morning she drove us to a diner where we sat across from each other, writing page after page in our composition books.

I hurt Sam a week later at a party. We saw one another from across the room, but I liked the attention my drunken rambling was getting from the doe-eyed boy poet who seemed to enjoy my flirting. I tried not to look at her again, and when she left she did not say goodbye.

I walked the five miles home that night, a bit drunk, after the boy poet had taken another girl to bed and the host had passed out in his dead grandfather's recliner. I had grown accustomed to walking, needing more distance the more tangled my thoughts were. Tonight though, worries and fears intertwined, like a ball of yarn that, the longer you work it, the tighter and more complicated the knots get. I stopped at the edge of the Sound to skip rocks, missing Noah, who had moved to California for college and never came home, who still sent me reading lists in the mail. He wanted me to go to school there, to come live with him. He said he would help me with the paperwork for grants and scholarships.

Early in the morning, the sky still dark, my phone rang and rang and when I ignored the ringing, it started up again.

"Hello?" Groggy, annoyed.

Mom, frantic, howling: *Oh my god, he's dead, what am I going to do? What am I going to do without him? He's gone oh my god he's gone.*

I froze. For too many breaths, I could not speak.

"Are you there? Eve, are you there?"

I was there, but not there, a behavior pattern worn deep into tissue and muscle.

"I'm here," I said, calm, caring. I fought back the other feelings, the flashbacks let loose by this sudden exit.

Ray died of a heart attack sometime in the night while Mom worked her shift at the hospital. He had been wearing a dirty gray T-shirt and boxers, his typical sleepwear. Mom walked in, placed her keys in the abalone shell dish at the front door like always. Seeing the lights were on all over the house, she called out. "Morning! Anybody up?"

She needed me. Of course I had to pack my things and take the bus home.

I arrived the next day.

In the living room, we sat next to one another, each sinking deeper and deeper into the brown suede sectional couch. Carmen, eight now, stared, motionless, perched in front of the television watching reruns. Mom continued her story after a sip of rum and coke I had made her, her third one, though she stayed sober and shocked.

"'Morning! Anybody up?' I called. And it was so quiet," she said. "It's never been that quiet. Thank god I didn't wake Carmen. The thought of her seeing what I saw…Oh, god."

I know what they mean now by blood-curdling scream, she said. White, she said. So pale, he had to be dead, but she knelt down and took his pulse on his wrist, then on his neck. Nothing. She turned him over and caught the scream in a gasp of despair this time. He looked blue or purple, like maybe he had already started to rot, though she knew that had to do with blood and gravity after the heart stops.

Mom slept on the couch that night, asked me to please leave the TV on. I took Carmen to bed, tucking her in. "Do you want me to read you a story?" I asked.

"That's okay," she said, her face blank, her eyes glazed, just like they had been in front of the television.

"I'm sorry about your Dad," I said.

"That's okay," she said, rolling over, tucking her pink heart-shaped pillow close.

I did not know what else to say. So I kissed her on the cheek, left her door cracked and the hall light on and went to sleep in my old room, now a spare room, part office, part storage space, part place to store all the crap my mom had impulse bought at buy-one-get-one-free sales: four giant packages of paper towels, three jackets of the same style in different colors, placed on top of two unopened DVD players. I could barely get to the bed without tripping over stuff. When I did reach the bed, I could not sleep.

The next morning over toast, bacon, and eggs I agreed to move back in to help Mom with Carmen.

"I'm warning you," Mom said. "She's wild. She doesn't listen. I thought Ray was going to kill her one of these days." A nervous laugh. She had not meant to say it that way. Under normal circumstances she would have filtered her thought, said something like *she drives Ray crazy because they are just alike*. She had let a tiny truth slip out. Too soon to tell if it was the beginning of more truth.

"Don't worry, Mom. It'll be fine. I'll help with Carmen."

I cleaned out my old room, talked Mom into a yard sale. Would she let me box up some things to put in the garage? We un-boxed one of the DVD players so Mom could watch rented movies on her nights off.

Carmen had black hair, black eyes, and an un-fillable pit of need. She pouted and whined. She clung to people, actually hung from their necks and arms like human jewelry. Mom left me with Carmen often, but I had little patience with her: I was mean.

When she asked me to read her a book I told her I was busy. I made up a story about how a ghost from the Great Depression haunted our house, then whenever the house creaked or a light flickered I would look at her bug-eyed and scared and say *what was that?* I told her the ghost was searching for her daughter, who starved to death because they had no money for food.

When she knocked on my bedroom door I yelled for her to go away, but she never seemed to get it.

These memories haunt me. I should have known better, been better. I came home to help with Carmen, but I pushed Carmen away at every turn. Still I am atoning for this sister failing.

There were other times though, when I softened, and I think now that those times built a bridge we could cross later when, as adults, we needed to get to the place where we could trust each other, love each other.

I started taking classes at the junior college because everyone thought I should. That first quarter I enrolled in poetry writing and philosophy, but I struggled to get to class and dropped out before the quarter ended.

I met a boy who told me I could write rivers of brilliant pages while he fished for gold if I followed him to Alaska. I left Mom and Carmen, easy as that.

We spent all the money we had between us to get there and to cover a couple months rent, which would not have been much, except that an uncle of his had died and left him an inheritance. We rented a studio apartment in Ketchikan. The plan was that he would work and I would stay home and write.

Two months passed and he had not found work, but I had. A waitress job that required a high tolerance for leering and public drunkenness. We consumed alcohol and each other, and always were naked and needing to be caressed. We watched *Wild At Heart* and he pointed out all his favorite scenes. We were reckless and lit and I forgot for that time that my own body had worth without him. Had I ever really known that? What does it mean to know? A seed had been planted, had sprouted and then seemingly shriveled, a dud. This body a thing to be taken, dug into, grabbed, admired and loathed, sometimes in two ticks of time.

Spinning, spinning, spinning.

Jill helped me find the abortion clinic in the phonebook, took me to the appointment when the day arrived. I had called her after arriving home from Alaska by bus, alone. As we pulled into the clinic lot, I expected to see crazies with *Abortion Kills* signs, maybe even have to force my way past them to get in. But the parking lot was near empty, autumn leaves blown by the wind skimming across its surface. Jill thought that maybe getting high would relax me. She must have noticed how I chewed on the inside of my cheek, itched my fingers, crossed and uncrossed my legs the whole trip there. She pulled her blue Nissan into a parking space way off in the corner of the lot. She loaded a big chunk of stinky weed, took a hit, held her breath, smiled and passed the glass pipe to me. I took a hit and, as I exhaled, felt my fear lighten if only for that moment.

"You can do this," Jill reassured.

"I did this," I said.

"Oh, for fuck sakes, Eve. Lay off yourself! It won't do any good."

"Right. Okay. You're right! Sorry. I better go in. It's time." I fumbled with the door handle.

"Do you want me to come in with you?" She asked.

"Nah, I got this, thanks. Just be here to pick me up." Tears held back, I wanted out of the car, to be on my way. I did not even wait for her to say she would be there. I needed to walk away in order to be able to do this at all.

The relaxation I felt sitting in the familiar comfort of Jill's car did not follow me into the clinic. I pushed the glass door and heard the bell announce my arrival. Fear seized my gut, and I felt I might vomit. The room seemed to be collapsing in on me, its imagery surreal and scary. The receptionist looked pasty white. The maroon lipstick on her white teeth and her wide, insistent smile scared me. I had reread every line of the forms at least twice, and yet still had two forms left. I felt as if this could not possibly be me sitting in this uncomfortable office chair beside this table stacked with old gossip magazines. I felt ashamed by all the leaflets for birth control methods stacked among the magazines and at the front counter.

I wrote. On paper, in the waiting room, I vowed that after this day things would be different. *I will be different. I will use my head.* My heart or my ego or whatever combination of both led me from one bad decision to the next and made me think that I could get away without

the normal consequences when one acts against their own knowledge of

what is true. I would be ruled by a cool head. I sat in this office waiting

for an abortion, I mused, because I had wanted him to love me. I had

gone against my better judgment, which told me he did not. Shame

flooded in so that I squirmed and kept checking my makeup in the silver

compact I carried in my purse, and biting the inside of my right cheek,

brow furrowed.

There was a picture of geese on the wall next to where I lay on a

butcher paper-covered exam table. Twelve birds—I had counted—flying

over a lake at sunset. I thought of Capitol Lake, of Dad, of what it must

feel like to fly, to honk to the world the way geese do.

More preparation than procedure made up the experience. The

thin cotton gown that did not conform to my body left my pale legs and

back exposed. The nurse practitioner showed casual confidence. I had the

impression she had performed this procedure countless times, was likely

to perform it many times more, and did not consider the role terribly

unlike the hygienist who scrapes plaque and teaches prevention. There

would be more today probably, right here in this room.

I watched her as she prepared to cleanse me of the possibility

of my becoming a parent. I scooted down the table when she cued me,

spread my legs, felt the coldness of her rubber-gloved hand she placed blandly on my knee. I was thinking in that moment of the invisible wall between me and everyone I had ever known. The wall behind which we hid our fear, our shame and also thought of how we tried to bridge the distance with talking and kissing. I thought, then, we are all just dying with each passing moment, and trying, in spite of that, to live.

What did one death matter in this human condition?

I felt a tug, and, almost immediate nausea, as the life that clung to my uterus was snuffed out.

It was done.

Get lots of rest, she said. Don't worry. There will be some bleeding. It's normal. Here's my card. Call if you have any questions. Do you have someone to drive you home?

Spinning, spinning, spinning.

NINE.

The boy from Alaska returns, and you move in together. The next
time, a year later, you insist on keeping the baby, swear you will do it on
your own if you have to. And you try, and that is some small part of what
destroys you two in the end. That and the bottles of booze collecting
in the recycling bin, the easy way you fall into enabling. It is amazing
how fast ten years can go, how easy it is to need less and less, give more
and more. But it is the body that marvels you most, how separate from
the self it can become, how it can be offered up so easily to be used by
someone else. And why? Fear of change, being alone, being unloved.
Because you'd never learned to love that body anyway, because it hadn't
ever been yours to love. You finish college and start your career as a high
school English teacher the same year your girls start kindergarten. You
master living in two worlds, two minds.

You are still doing yoga, you even sign up for a class, and there is something there you want but can not quite get to. Then one day when your girls are napping, you put on some tennis shoes and you go for a run. You go out the next day and the next. You join a group of other women who write. You sign up for a marathon, look up a training plan online and begin. When the long runs get really long, you wake up at five and run for three hours, more.

It is a cool, sunny October day in San Francisco the day you run. The boy from Alaska stands with your girls at mile 21 waiting for you to run by, and when you get there, you want to fall into them, beg them to carry you home. Then you smell his boozy breath and you remember how last night he got you kicked out of the restaurant you'd made reservations for three months in advance. You run on. When you cross the finish line, there is nothing left of your body, you have burned through it all and the tears unlock themselves from their dungeons and trample you.

You join a group of other women who run. You go back to school to write fiction. You are creating your greatest work and you do not even know it yet. It is not made of words, it is made of breath, yours, and muscle and bone and flesh. It is not pretty when you tell the boy from Alaska to go, to not come back. You can feel the web of lies ripping as if it were the fibers of your very beings and he would like to leave you crushed by his words if he can. But the seed was planted for this, and you did nurture it, you did. And so it sprouts and blooms and you climb its stem up to the clouds and into a new story: your own.

TEN.

I rarely think about that geese painting, the little death that happened there. I know people whose sad stories get stuck on repeat in their heads. Suffering becomes so familiar they seem to know no other way. They fill their present and their future with past woes, leaving no room for change.

When I have occasion to tell the darker parts of my past, people tell me how resilient I am. They cannot believe that I have "come so far" because the prevailing wisdom is that drunks raise drunks and people who get beat as children grow up to beat their children.

That kind of lie has drowned so many of us.

In the recurring nightmare I still sometimes have, I cannot move and I cannot speak. When I wake, I feel grateful I know how it feels to run full speed over roots and rocks and through light-illuminated evergreens, to arc and sink in cobra pose or plow pose, to dive into and swim through cool lake water in summer, to sit still, observing each fantastic breath. Hallelujah! To put pen to blank page and let words loose, or to make words out of many separate keystrokes. To say I am sorry, I love you. To dance and laugh with my sisters, who understand.

Three months ago, Carmen and I went hiking together to Enchanted Valley in Olympic National Park. She brought her girlfriend Meg and I brought my twins. They are eleven and only had to carry day packs with their clothes and sleeping bags. I carried the tent, the stove, the food (heaviest) and other supplies we were sure we would need (and in some cases did).

In the early part of the hike, I struggled more than I expected to, as sometimes happens no matter how many miles you have traveled in boots or running shoes. Your lungs and legs can be strong and still you might hit the smallest incline, lungs small, muscles burning. In these cases, it is the breath that carries you. Fortunately, Meg had never hiked more than a few miles on city trails and needed to stop often, so she was my excuse to go slow.

"Sorry I'm slowing you down," she apologized, her young skin pink, glowing.

"No worries," I said. "We're not in a race." I put my hand on a giant cedar stump and felt it give in to my weight, like a pillow.

At O'Neil Creek we stopped for lunch. Only half way, we all were losing confidence, our mouths dry, our shoulders and quads burning. The adults, that is. The girls with their light packs bounced along, paused to skip rocks when we came upon the river, and made up stories to the beat of their walking sticks.

We had subsisted nearly five hours on trail mix and electrolyte gummies, and were eager to have a real meal. Meg pulled out the two ham and cheese sandwiches on rye bread she had made for Carmen and herself, along with a big bag of sour cream and onion potato chips. I watched the way she offered Carmen the food, the way their hands brushed, and I felt glad for Carmen.

"This is way harder than I thought it would be." Meg leaned back against a log, took a swig from her wide-mouthed water bottle.

"It's not easy," I agreed, wiping my brow and getting up to bring the girls their peanut butter honey and banana sandwiches. They sat several feet away, jabbering about fairy houses.

"Oh, you're just humoring me," Meg said, as I returned. "This can't be hard for you. Your sister told me you've run a marathon."

"Yes. And that was hard, too. Worth it, though."

We ate and we napped, the midday sun shining boldly through the trees, though it'd been sprinkling only an hour before.

By the time we made it the valley, we'd spotted a black bear in the distance. I had needed four cheerleaders to cross a log over an arm of the river, and we had stopped to pump water six times. When we descended into the valley the sun had not yet set and the walls of waterfalls surrounding us caught the light, shimmered.

After unburdening themselves of their packs and putting their tents up, Meg and Carmen went off on a river walk together.

The girls found a patch of grass to lie down on while I lit up the stove and boiled shrimp fettuccine in a vacuum-sealed pouch. When the food was ready I called them all back to me and we ate until our bellies were full. Then we said our goodnights and I stumbled off into my tent to rest my tired body.

As I fell asleep, I counted breaths, blessings.

I woke stiff and sore, stood with Carmen and Meg sipping camp-dark coffee, watching the steam lift and disappear with the rising sun. The girls dozed, dreamed in the tent.

Meg made the suggestion, maybe not even really meaning it.

"I bet that river water would feel refreshing. Cold, but refreshing."

The idea caught in each of us, so that we found ourselves ambling barefoot over sharp river rocks to get the edge of the water, waded in a step or two, feet sinking into the silt.

We swam in a place where the river pooled and stalled. We marched through the flowing river to get there, using each other's shoulders for balance along the way. I pinched my nose and dipped down, counted slowly to ten, shot up for air, brushed the water up my face with my hands.

Our laughter echoed through the valley, echoes in my memory, adds to the moments, more of them every day, where I inhabit this body and live free.

www.ingramcontent.com/pod-product-compliance
Lightning Source LLC
Chambersburg PA
CBHW060231180626
46813CB00007B/3043